# DAYS OF PANIC: EMP Survival Series Book 1

JACK HUNT

DIRECT RESPONSE PUBLISHING

ISBN-13: 978-1983907869
ISBN-10: 1983907863

**Also By Jack Hunt**

*The Renegades*
*The Renegades 2: Aftermath*
*The Renegades 3: Fortress*
*The Renegades 4: Colony*
*The Renegades 5: United*
*Mavericks: Hunters Moon*
*Killing Time*
*State of Panic*
*State of Shock*
*State of Decay*
*Defiant*
*Phobia*
*Anxiety*
*Strain*
*Blackout*
*Darkest Hour*
*Final Impact*
*And Many More…*

## Dedication

For my family.

# Chapter 1

New York City

Twelve Hours Before

Jesse Michaels couldn't believe his bad luck. There were a lot of upsides to being a bike messenger in the Big Apple but being held up at gunpoint wasn't one. Twelve months of pedaling through the city that never slept, it was only a matter of time before a group of hoodlums decided to jump him and lighten his load, he just didn't expect it on the busiest day of the year. In all truth he'd wondered why it hadn't occurred sooner.

The three thugs surrounded him like a pack of wolves while the meanest leaned in and pressed the Glock's cold, hard muzzle to his forehead.

The guy's brow pinched. "Run that by me again?"

Without hesitation or fear Jesse replied, "You heard me. No."

The guy looked baffled. He obviously wasn't used to hearing that, especially not when they had a guy like him outnumbered and out of sight of anyone who might come to his aid. He pushed the gun harder against Jesse's head and eyeballed him.

"You wanna die?"

There it was, the question he'd been chewing on for the past twelve months since losing Chloe. To be honest, he really hadn't made up his mind. He certainly had no fear of death. Whether he died today or checked out in fifty years' time, it was unavoidable.

He never answered the question.

"Is the contents of the bag really worth losing your head over? Huh?"

"I guess you'll need to pull the trigger to find out," Jesse replied.

He snorted and cast a glance at his two pals. He shot them a look of disbelief before returning to the reason they'd jumped him and dragged him into a urine-smelling back alley full of industrial dumpsters and winos. In a split second the thug reared his hand back and whipped Jesse across the face knocking him off his bike. Then he leaned over to take what he wanted by force.

"Give me that," he said, shoving Jesse and tearing off the backpack while the other two prevented him from resisting. "I gotta say, man, you are either the dumbest asshole in the city or you have serious mental issues. Either way, I would recommend getting your head examined."

He tapped the muzzle against Jesse's black bicycle helmet.

The guy unzipped the bag, peered inside, grinned and jerked his head to let the others know to follow him. "Nice doing business with you." One of his pals kicked his bike. Then the other one picked it up and tossed it into a dumpster. It clanged and echoed. They laughed and disappeared into the stream of pedestrians and the steam rising from manhole covers. Why they'd bothered to target him was a mystery. They couldn't have got away with much. Most of his runs were for law firms and corporate offices — material that couldn't be faxed, emailed, scanned or FedExed. Contrary to what most might have thought, bike messengers were still needed. It was cheap, fast, and a reliable service. It catered to the "I want it now" generation. And there was no way anyone could get something from point A to point B in the city faster than a bike messenger. Racking up anywhere from 40 to 60 miles a day, he could eat whatever the hell he liked as it burned off like wildfire. He worked for no one, but contracted himself out like the other five thousand bike messengers in New York. When he wasn't doing runs for City Kings, he filled up his day with runs for UberRUSH, GrubHub, Postmates, DoorDash, and some flower firms. While the work was simple, he was lucky to make eighty bucks on a good day. It certainly was a far cry from the work he'd previously done.

Jesse coughed and rubbed the side of his eye that was beginning to swell.

He looked towards the mouth of the alley where a slew of pedestrians hurried about their day. He spat a wad of blood on the ground before gazing up at the gray sky. It was freezing cold in December. The streets were packed. New Year's Eve was a nightmare. Over one million lunatics crammed into Times Square every year just to scream, kiss and see that damn glittering ball drop. It was utter madness and the reason Jesse had been trying to get wrapped up by three that afternoon. He didn't want to get stuck in the middle of it; it brought back too many bad memories. The cops were already closing down access to Times Square starting with 43rd Street and Broadway then working their way north as thousands from out of the city arrived. On one hand the lack of vehicle traffic made it easy to weave through the streets but with the boys in blue out, it meant fewer rules could be broken — like skitching, which involved latching onto a vehicle, or blowing through red lights because stopping meant a delivery might not arrive on time.

Jesse remained on the ground for a second or two before clambering to his feet and brushing off the city grime. He brought a sleeve up to his arm and smelled it, it reeked of piss. "Shit." He grimaced and went over to the dumpster and leaned in to fish his bike out. After dragging it out and wiping off pasta, and God knows what else, he looked at the back wheel which was wonky. He straightened it out as best as he could and then prepared to make a call to Alfonzo, the head boss at City Kings.

Leaning his bike up against the dumpster, he retrieved his phone and placed the call. The fact that those three thugs hadn't stolen his phone, or the six dollars in pocket change, made him think they knew what was in the bag. They'd probably been paid by some big shot to ensure it didn't arrive at its location. Delays in the city could make or break businesses. It could bring court cases to a grind and cause no end of trouble as it was an easy way to make other people's lives a living hell.

"Jesse, where the hell are you? Doug Richards hasn't got his package."

"Yeah, about that."

"Why don't I like the sound of that?"

Jesse rubbed his eye again. It hurt like hell.

"I was jumped."

"Noooo," Alfonzo replied.

"Nothing I could do about it. Three of them, one had a gun. They took everything."

Alfonzo sighed.

"Look, don't worry about it. I got them on camera."

"What?" Alfonzo asked.

"I've been wearing a GoPro lately. You know, to record my daily route."

"Why?"

"Because I'm not exactly rolling in money, and strangely enough people are interested in seeing what I do for a living. I upload it online and make a few bucks on ads. Anyway, those guys couldn't have been too bright as they never bothered to search me. They just wanted the bag."

Jesse groaned and steadied himself against the dumpster.

"You okay?"

"A few scratches and bruises. I'll live."

"Right."

There was dead air between them.

"Alfonzo."

"Yeah. Um. Look, just head to the next pickup location. I'll deal with this."

"The next pickup? Have you seen it out here? The streets are crawling with people. I'll be lucky if I can make it a few blocks. It's crazy. Anyway, I was planning on knocking off early. Besides my bike isn't exactly in the best state." He stared down at the wheel. That was one of the downsides to being a bike messenger. You had to buy your own bike, replace tires, maintain it, get the right clothes. There were no promotions or raises, no healthcare, no workers compensation and every day he had to risk his neck dealing with pedestrians and annoyed cab drivers. Every month bike messengers were injured by collisions or doors swinging open, and some even died. That's why there was such a high turnover. With the low rate of pay, no one got into this to make money, it was all about freedom, or in Jesse's case, healing, as it was the only thing that allowed his mind to stay off the past.

"Two more pickups and drop-offs. C'mon, you owe me that."

"Owe you?" Jesse asked.

"Jesse, I'm on the hook for everything that was lost. Someone has to take responsibility."

"Just give the cops my video footage."

"Doesn't matter. Listen, just do the last two pickups or…"

"Or what? I don't work for you, Alfonzo."

"No, you don't, but you rely on the work I send your way."

He was right of course. The pickings were slim in the city. Big courier companies were becoming a thing of the past with more and more deliveries being sent by email.

However, with advancements in technology, laziness had become the new problem, and some companies were taking advantage of that by offering free pickup and delivery, and then making their money off the back end through sponsors and other forms of advertising. Jesse was starting to feel like a walking billboard with ads attached to his clothing.

"How much?" Jesse asked. Every online messenger service was different. Some might offer sixty to seventy percent per delivery, but when the delivery cost was only five bucks, you had to chase the money to make it. That's why he preferred working with Alfonzo, he could haggle with him and City Kings had been around long before all the new startup companies showed up on the scene.

"Thirty bucks."

"Sixty," Jesse replied.

"Forty."

"Fifty-five."

"Forty!"

He groaned. "Alright, I'll do it."

"Good man. Oh, and Jesse. Happy New Year."

"Yeah, yeah." Jesse grunted and pursed his lips together as he got back on his bike and wobbled off down the alleyway back into the maze of death.

* * *

He grunted at the sight. The line was longer than last time. He hated waiting because it meant talking to people but he had little choice as the other places would be just as bad. Elliot Wilson pushed his shopping cart full of cans, bottles and other plastics to one side then fished around in his pocket for a cigarette and lit it. He blew a plume of gray smoke and squinted as he scanned the dirty faces of fellow street people while he waited outside one of the Acme markets in Manhattan. It was one of several supermarkets, drugstores, and other businesses registered as redemption centers, and had become his single source of income after arriving in the city over a year ago. He'd spent the better part of the morning and early afternoon collecting sticky containers from trash receptacles, as each one would net him five cents, and allow him to redeem the legal maximum of $12 per visit. Most homeless New Yorkers would go from one supermarket to the next and if they were lucky, they might be able to scrape together just enough to make it through to the next day. Canning was unpredictable and could be dangerous at times, but it was all he could rely on. The street was full of the mentally unstable, those who wouldn't think twice about sticking a blade in you to steal what you had. For him, thieving was out of the question, and no one would hire him — not without a fixed residence. Besides, he hadn't come to the city to find work, but that was another story.

Elliot hopped up on top of the shopping cart and pulled out a *New York Post* newspaper he'd swiped from a McDonald's restaurant earlier that morning. The headline read: *North Korea Launches Ballistic Missile Hours After White House Warning.* He scanned the article which covered the president in a UN speech threatening to attack and totally destroy North Korea. There had been mixed opinions from the American people on what should or shouldn't be done. Some felt the president was only inciting the young leader of North Korea.

"Can I bum a cigarette?" a gruff voice asked.

Elliot lifted his eyes. It was the same question every time. While he saw many of the same faces, and some tried to speak with him, for the most part he kept to himself. It was safer that way. There was no telling whom he was dealing with, the nicest of people could turn ugly in seconds. Had he met the guy down in the underground he would have obliged but standing here, in a line of nine, that was like flashing a handful of money. Instead, he just shook his head. "Sorry, last one."

"Too bad. Then a drag?"

He was persistent. Hustling, everyone had to do it. Elliot scanned the man behind him, and the woman in front, before handing him the partially smoked cigarette.

"Keep it."

The grizzled homeless man gave a nod. "Thanks, man."

He went back to reading the article. According to the military, the North Koreans already had a ballistic missile submarine capable of causing major damage but rumors has it they had developed a more advanced one that would present an even greater challenge to the USA. *China suspected of helping the North Koreans develop the technology?* He shook his head. He wouldn't put it past them.

Ahead of him a commotion had started between a woman and a guy. It was common to see arguments. One person would steal a bag of cans from another or accuse someone of having scavenged in their territory. He dropped the newspaper back into the cart and watched as the white male shoved the small Chinese woman to the ground and everyone looked on without saying or doing a thing. Only one guy tried to intervene but after the man flashed a blade he backed off with his hands up. It was a dog-eat-dog world. It reminded him of wolves attacking prey. The dominant ones would prevent the others from coming close until they had fed.

"Those are mine," she said, tears streaking down her face.

"I saw you this morning. I warned you not to come into my neighborhood," he said taking what she had and loading it into his already overfilled cart. He had them in bags hanging off the sides and tied to the back. Elliot watched the woman claw her way back to her feet and try to retrieve her bags. This time the man kicked her hard in the stomach knocking her back. He loomed over her, jabbing his finger in her face. "You brought this upon yourself." Then he began mocking her by pretending to sob. "Now shut the hell up."

As he turned to continue robbing her, Elliot hit him square on the end of the nose. It burst like a fire hydrant and he buckled but remained standing. One more crack to the jaw and he was out cold. Then, without saying a word, Elliot took the bags he'd taken from the woman and placed them back in her cart, then went over and took her hand and helped her up.

"Go, find another place to redeem the cans and bottles."

She nodded and hurried off with the cart, shortening

the line. Elliot returned to his spot in the line and kept an eye on the man who was lying near his cart. He figured he wouldn't be out for long and when he awoke things would get even more violent, but he wasn't going to run. That was a sign of weakness; besides, he still had $12 to collect.

After redeeming his cash, he headed back to Grand Central Terminal; his home was located underneath the platform between tracks 111 and 112 on the lower level. He could have stayed in a shelter and for the first day after arriving in the city he had, that was until he woke up to some naked guy jacking off near his face. Shelters were ripe with the mentally ill. If it wasn't dealing with sexual advances, it was the risk of being stabbed or suffocated at night. It was brutal, and the reason why so many preferred to sleep on the sidewalks, huddled below blankets, or down in the tunnels where the air was humid and poor. It was better than dealing with shelter curfews, restrictive laws and a broken social system.

There, he and other homeless people referred to as

mole people created homes in a labyrinth of graffiti-filled tunnels, above dirty support beams and inside small abandoned crew rooms that were at one time used by tunnel workers. Elliot had managed to turn his dusty abode into a two-room residence complete with an old mattress, cookware, blankets, and even a camping stove and mini fridge that pirated electricity from somewhere in the underground system.

Although the tunnels were safer than shelters, the real threat came from the Amtrak Police who would go out of their way to clear him and the others out on a daily basis. So far, he'd managed to elude them. In the first few months after he'd moved below ground some of the Amtrak Police had been kind enough to treat him and others with respect and escort them out, but others were brutal in their eviction, destroying the little they had. To them, they were less than human — nothing more than scavengers living off the grid, hidden beneath rowdy streets and carved avenues and beyond the rules of society.

Elliot waited on the platform like any other commuter,

though it wasn't the train he was waiting to get into, it was the tunnel. He always had to move fast or there was a risk of being caught. A warm breeze of air blew out of the mouth of the tunnel that was wide and dark, swallowing the light and all that was good. The smell of brake dust and mold lingered in the air. He gazed down at the rubble littering the train tracks, and rats scouring for food, then back at the crowd as they began to board the next train. After a few seconds of hesitation he hopped down and jogged on into the darkness, gravel crunching below his boots. The city growled overhead through the cracks and vents, muffled by the concrete. As he moved down the tunnel, his eyes adjusting to the darkness, a few faces appeared to see if he was the Amtrak Police. Upon recognizing Elliot, they disappeared into their holes. He'd met them all. The mentally ill, the bipolar, the jobless, the substance abuser, the thief and those just looking to escape a world caught up in pursuit of material accumulation and social acceptance.

"Hey Elliot!"

A man he'd come to know as Squid sat on the edge of a wall, his legs dangling off as he drank a beer.

"How are yah?" Elliot asked.

He raised his beer. "Could be better, could be worse." It was the same answer he gave every time. "Listen, I wouldn't head down there today. I saw them rooting around near your place."

"Shit!" Elliot didn't have any problem with the homeless walking through his place as he hid his valuable items in different places in the underground but Amtrak, the very mention of them riled him up. He'd had to move three times over the past year, and the last place had been near perfect. Perfect for an underground home.

"You want a drink?" He offered Elliot a beer, but he declined and pressed on passing stained walls and foul-smelling areas of the tunnel until he came to the turning that led down to his spot. The flicker of shadows coming from fire against the walls and the stench of smoke didn't sit well with him. A glance around the corner confirmed his fears. Someone had set fire to his possessions. It wasn't the Amtrak cops, they didn't know he was there. He'd been really discreet this time around. It had to have been one of the other tunnel dwellers. There were many that were jealous, disgruntled or would lash out if they found nothing of value.

"Hey you there!" An Amtrak cop's flashlight beam washed over Elliot's face, snapping him out of the past. Elliot backed up. "Stop!" they yelled.

But he didn't wait. It was one thing to be evicted, another to be charged with vandalism. They wouldn't care who they grabbed so long as they had someone to pin it on. Elliot turned and double-timed it out, heading for topside. *Shit!* he muttered under his breath. Now he had to kill time until he could return. He figured he would join others in Times Square, seek out the most valuable spots where thousands of cans and bottles were thrown, and then maybe tomorrow he could find a new spot and rebuild.

He punched a wall with the side of his hand.

It was all gone. Everything wiped out.

He reached into his pocket and fished out the one thing that meant the most to him — a photo. Even in the darkness he could make out their faces although the snapshot had become dirtied and wrinkled at the corners. His heart ached for days gone by and the man he was before returning from war.

## Chapter 2

Damon Miles slammed the pay phone down hard after getting no answer. It was the third time he'd tried phoning him. He shivered and tucked his hands into his pockets, trying to stay warm as his breath rose above like a ghostly apparition. He'd been promised a ride at four-thirty that morning after being dropped off by the blue and white correctional bus from Rikers Island along with 40 other cheering inmates. Conversation on the ride that morning circulated around girls and drugs, mostly drugs. It was how they coped. It was what got them through the stretch inside. His mood had been upbeat that morning, but that all changed when there was no one there to greet him.

*Where the hell are you, Cole?* he thought.

He'd watched the others holding brown paper bags filled with their belongings head off in different directions. The only light that morning came from a

Twin Donut shop, a subway station and the cell phones of several prostitutes who were leaning against a wall expecting to make a quick buck. Damon fished out what he had left. In his hand was fifty cents. Those who didn't have money when they left were given $4.25, enough to grab themselves a cup of coffee and maybe a ride to somewhere else in the city. He'd already used his on cheap coffee, a donut and multiple phone calls.

As he stood at the corner of Jackson Avenue and Queens Plaza South, he felt like a fish out of water. It wasn't meant to be like this. He'd lost so much time being inside, never mind that part of him that had broken down through the day-to-day routine of prison life. Now under any other circumstances he might have been pissed off, but he was free, and that was all that mattered. The rest was just details. He could find his way home if need be, but he'd been holding out hope of a ride. They at least owed him that after he took the fall. He glanced at a clock through the donut store window. It was closing in on three o'clock in the afternoon. He'd been standing there in the cold for eleven hours, hoping that Cole would arrive, but after getting no answer on his phone he figured he'd forgotten, or he didn't want to be associated with him anymore. Either way it wasn't good. He exhaled hard and cast his eyes across the street to where a few homeless individuals scavenged through garbage. The thought of finding a different job after having his record tainted bore down on him like a heavy weight.

A black girl with red dreadlocks, tight pants and a white blouse made her way over with two friends, swaying her ass from side to side. She snapped her lips, chewing gum and blowing bubbles.

"Hey darling, you looking for a warm bed for the night? We can see the New Year in together."

He smiled. "Sounds good."

"How much you got?"

"What will fifty cents get me?" He grinned, knowing full well she was about to shoot him down. They were cheap but not that cheap. He'd heard a few of the guys saying they offered sexual favors from $30 to $50. Only a few who left the prison could afford it, the rest were just hoping to butter them up with sweet talk. Not him. He wasn't serious. He was just playing with her. Sure he was desperate for some female companionship, but he wouldn't touch a prostitute with a barge pole. That was just damn nasty.

She laughed. "You come back once you've earned some green."

"Oh, c'mon, don't you want to talk?"

"Money is time, honey, and I don't have much of either and neither do you."

"I got all the time in the world."

She ran a hand over his face teasing him before brushing past and continuing on her way. Damon stood there for a few more minutes until he decided that Cole wasn't coming, and he wasn't going to spend the night freezing to death beneath the hulking train pylons of Queens Plaza. As he stepped off the curb onto the grime-filled streets heading for Queensborough Bridge, he figured he would head for Times Square. There was sure to be more than enough people caught up in the countdown of the ball drop that he'd be able to pick a few pockets and earn enough cash for a Greyhound bus home.

* * *

"Sir, would you stop yelling at me?" Maggie Gray said leaning back in her seat. She adjusted the headset and glanced around at the other three hundred customer support reps taking shit from technical neophytes. These were people who shouldn't have ever bought a computer in the first place, or at least should have read the warranty fine print before phoning her. Her job was pretty simple. Click a button, take a call, assist someone having problems with their computer, take notes, end the call and repeat that for eight hours straight. She worked all kinds of shifts and last year she had seen in the New Year while talking to some eighty-year-old woman in Florida who couldn't start her computer because she hadn't even plugged the damn thing in. Of course she hadn't found that out until she'd been on the phone with her for forty minutes.

Now she was getting an earful from some self-righteous prick who'd misunderstood the warranty associated with his computer and wasn't willing to work with her to go through a format and reinstall.

"I want you to get up right now and tell your supervisor that I want a word with him."

"Unfortunately, we don't have any supervisors here today. They all left at three," Maggie replied.

"Bullshit. I want this piece of crap replaced with a new computer."

"Sir, if you would listen to me for a moment, I can get this all fixed up in less than twenty minutes."

"Twenty minutes? Do you honestly think I have twenty minutes?"

People were so damn impatient. Everything had to be instant. With advancements in technology and a million and one things vying for people's attention, it had created a new generation of lazy ass idiots who had lost the art of savoring life. If it didn't work, they wanted a replacement not a fix. If it didn't thrill them from the start, they wanted to toss it. If they couldn't get it now, they went elsewhere. She'd heard every sob story under the sun over the phone. Now, she considered herself a patient person but even she had her limits.

"Sir, everyone else has to go through the same thing as you."

Maggie had been a technical customer service rep for Dell Computers for the past three years. The number of reps had dwindled over the years as Dell handed support over to offshore companies whose employees could barely speak English, but the company she worked for still had a contract with Dell. They were the last of a dying breed, her friend Lexi said. She spun in her chair and eyed Lexi. They didn't need to say anything to each other; they both knew when the other was dealing with a difficult customer.

"Are you going to help or not?" the guy bellowed.

"I just told you."

"Shut up. You don't tell me anything, bitch. Get up

now and get me a support rep before I get you fired."

She could take a lot from a customer but she drew the line at being called a bitch.

"You know, pal, with one click of a button I could send your ass to Mexico for support."

"You do that and…"

She leaned forward. Click.

"Happy New Year, asshole," she said over the line that was now dead.

Yeah, she could have lost her job over it, but she'd just about had enough of that guy bellyaching. Besides, she was already five minutes past the end of her shift. Usually they were required to take phone calls up to the last minute of their shift but that meant she could land a call that would send her into overtime and this job didn't pay enough to warrant staying more than five minutes longer.

"I wondered when you were going to dump his ass," Lexi said tossing off her headset and logging out of her phone. Maggie started shutting down her computer and tossed her water bottle into her backpack.

"I was just waiting for the right moment."

"He called you a bitch, didn't he?"

"Yep!" she said without even looking at her.

"So you're coming with me tonight?"

"Uh, I don't know, Lexi."

"Come on. Do you really want to see the New Year in alone at home?"

"I'm not alone."

"Right, you have your fish."

"It's all the company I need."

"Brad's going to be there."

Maggie smiled. "Lexi. How many times have I told you? I'm not interested."

"You might not be but he is. He still talks about you."

Lexi had tricked her into going out a month ago, only to find out that she'd arranged a double date and told Brad Wilerman that Maggie was interested in him. It had been the most awkward dinner date she'd ever been on. He was a nice enough guy — good looking, a secure job as a banker and no baggage, but he was as boring as hell.

All he ever went on about was his job. It was like nothing else existed in the world. Lexi had been trying to play matchmaker for the past year after Maggie had cut ties with Eric, her boyfriend of two years.

"Lexi, I have a few things to do."

"Like what? You are going to order in Chinese, watch a teary-eyed movie and wake up and wish you had been with us. Admit it."

"Actually I was thinking of going for seafood tonight."

"Maggie!"

Silence stretched between them before Lexi scooped up her bag and they headed out. Maggie waved to a few of her colleagues and wished them a Happy New Year before swiping out.

"You run into Eric lately?" Lexi asked.

"He showed up at my place three days ago, drunk out of his mind. I had to call the cops."

"How did he find you?"

"That's what I would like to know."

"Really, you should move into the apartment across

from me. At least then if he shows up I can be there to help, or Matt can."

Eric had been a pain in the ass since they'd broken up. He'd never once laid a hand on her in the two years they'd been together, then that all changed when he started accusing her of seeing another guy. It was out of character for him. Anyway, she wore a black eye for two weeks, and had to listen to his apologies about never doing it again before she made the decision to leave him. Even then she had to leave in the middle of the night because he'd watch her every move. She was even convinced he had followed her on the few times she'd gone out with Lexi.

"Yeah, I might take you up on that."

"Listen, we'll head back to your place. You can grab a few items. Stay at my place tonight as we're going to get back late. How's that sound?"

"And my fish?"

She laughed. "I think they'll survive."

She gripped her arm as they walked across the parking

lot. A cold wind nipped at her ears and she pulled in her coat. Being outside on a cold night like this wasn't her idea of fun. But that was Lexi's style. She couldn't stay still for a minute. She had to be the center of attention. She had to be right there in the middle of the action otherwise she felt she was missing out. Lexi flipped her long red hair, her heels clicking against the sidewalk.

"You were already there last year. Why go again?" Maggie asked.

"It's going to be different this year."

"How so?"

"You'll see."

"Lexi, you know I hate surprises."

"That's why I'm not telling you," Lexi said with a grin as she retrieved her keys from her purse and pressed the key fob to unlock her red Toyota Prius. It took them twenty minutes to arrive at her one-bedroom apartment in Bushwick. Lexi lived over in Williamsburg with her fiancé Matt. The two of them had been together for close to six years. As they pulled up outside, Maggie did her usual check of looking up and down the road for Eric's SUV before getting out.

"You want me to come inside?" Lexi yelled from her car as she pulled ahead.

"No, I'll just be a few minutes."

Maggie double-timed it up the steps and pushed open the doors which led into an apartment block that had four apartments, two on the lower floor and two above. She checked her mailbox first before heading upstairs. There was nothing but bills. It hadn't been easy living alone, and she hadn't told her parents about Eric hitting her. They'd already been against her moving to the city after she turned twenty-two but there were no jobs in the small town of Andale, Kansas. At least not the kind that she was after. She'd studied media in the hopes of getting involved in TV but it hadn't worked out. It was all about who you knew and besides Lexi and Matt, she didn't know anyone else in New York. She'd even thought about moving home after the whole incident with Eric but Lexi had managed to talk her out of it. She'd even helped her land a job at the call center. Things will improve, she said. And for a few months she thought maybe they would until Eric tracked her down.

Maggie jammed the key into the lock and let herself into her apartment. It wasn't much to look at, just a simple one-bedroom place, hardwood floors, open kitchen with just enough furniture and living space to entertain two other people. She tossed her bag on the couch and went over and fed the fish, crumbling a few pieces of food into the bowl. She'd named her two fish after the old comedy actors Laurel and Hardy.

"Hey guys, I'm gonna be out for the night. Don't wait up."

She went about stuffing a small backpack with a fresh outfit of clothing, some makeup and toiletries. Maggie was in the bathroom when she heard the front door creak open.

"I know, I'm taking forever. Be right there, Lexi."

She was so caught up in gathering what she needed that she didn't think to check. Not that it would have helped. She heard the door close and the lock click, that's when she poked her head out. "Lexi?"

"We need to talk, Maggie."

Her stomach dropped. It was Eric.

"What are you doing here?"

"You don't return my phone calls. You've got the police involved. All I want to do is talk."

She came out and went to get her belongings. Eric stood there, six foot three, a rugged-looking individual who had played football all through high school. Dark hair, chiseled jaw and far bigger than she was. She'd met him in her first year of film school. Back then he seemed fine. "We are done talking, now get out before I call the cops," she yelled.

"Oh, Maggie, why have you got to say that?"

She stabbed her finger at him. "It's over between us. Now get out!"

"No it's not. You haven't given me a chance."

She went to slip by him and he shifted to the left and blocked her.

"You got one chance, and you screwed it up," she replied.

Her father had always told her that any guy she dated would make mistakes. That wasn't an issue. Mistakes could be corrected, even forgiven, but if any man raised a hand to her, that was it. It was over. There was no second chance. She agreed.

Eric looked at her bag and tried to grab it out of her hands.

"Where are you going?"

"None of your damn business."

"So you seeing someone now?" he asked in an accusing manner.

"No. But even if I was, what has that got to do with you?"

He grabbed her by the arm and squeezed tight.

"Listen to me."

"Let go, Eric!" She struggled within his grasp.

"Why do you have to act like such a bitch?"

Maybe that's why she reacted so fiercely to the word.

She'd never been called that by anyone until Eric.

"Please. Let go of my arm."

"And you'll listen to me?"

"Let go."

"Not until you listen."

She knew she wasn't going to get anywhere by struggling. He had at least a hundred pounds on her and one swipe from the back of his hand and she'd be seeing stars. She stopped resisting and looked at him. "What do you want?"

"You. Me. This," he said staring around at the apartment. "I messed up. I'm sorry. I won't do it again. I've been doing a lot of thinking lately. You know, about you and me and I know we can make this work. You'll see."

While he was talking she was eyeing a vase on the counter. She'd never been one for violence but after he hit her, she had sworn that if he ever came near her again, it would be the last time. Eric continued, "I can move in tonight. I'll take you to Times Square. It will be like old times."

Another reason why she didn't want to go there, he'd taken her there several years in a row while they were dating and once after he moved in. Everything about the noise, the people and the event just reminded her of him.

"So, what do you think?"

She pursed her lips and tried to crack a faint smile then shrugged. As soon as he released his grip, she would go for it.

"Maggie?"

"I don't know, Eric."

"Come on, you know when things were good they were good."

"Yeah, um…" She pulled away from him. "Okay."

He got this wild grin on his face like he'd just hit the lottery, and then he released her. "Ah, you'll see. I knew it. You and I, we got something that is far stronger than…"

Before he could finish, she reached for the ceramic vase full of wildflowers and smashed it over his head. He let out this wild cry, and she bolted for the door. She unlocked the multiple latches then swung the door open. Before she had a foot outside, she felt a hand grasp the back of her hair and pull her back in. She slid across the glossy hardwood floor and her shoulder banged into a small side table knocking it over. She felt a shot of pain and reached up to find her head was bleeding.

If that wasn't bad enough, Eric was fuming. He kicked over a chair and swiped his hand across the counter knocking the fishbowl to the ground. Glass shattered and her fish slid across the floor. She was in too much pain and shock to even react. All she could do was look on in a state of panic.

"Now look what you made me do!" he bellowed.

"Help!" she screamed, hoping one of the neighbors would hear her but no one did. It was the middle of the day. If people weren't at work, they were probably out on the streets joining with all the other revelers. She knew Lexi was outside. Maggie spotted her cell phone on the table across the room. If she could reach that, she could call the cops. Eric followed her gaze and went over and snatched it up and tossed it at the window. He must have thought it would just bounce off, instead it shattered the window. Scrambling to her feet she tried to make a beeline for the door, but he burst across the room and knocked her sideways into the wall. She hit it with such force that the drywall buckled and she collapsed to the floor gasping for air. Eric loomed over her, his face twisting into someone she didn't even recognize. Was this even the same man she'd met years ago? What had changed? Surely there should have been signs. Red flags? No, he wasn't like this when she first met him. He was the sweetest man she'd ever met.

"All you had to do was give me another chance."

He stabbed his finger near her face. Crying, she choked on her tears. "Get out, Eric. I'm going to call the cops."

"The cops aren't coming. It's New Year's Eve, stupid!"

Between his legs she saw Lexi coming up behind him. She screamed at Eric to mask the sound of her approaching. She had no idea what Lexi was going to do but just seeing her made her feel better. Eric had opened his mouth to continue his tirade when his whole body started to vibrate. He hit the ground and started flapping around like a fish out of water while Lexi held a Taser against the back of his neck.

"You fucking asshole!" She looked at Maggie. "Maggie, move, now. Go to my car."

Maggie didn't hesitate, she got up, grabbed her bag and keys, and glanced once at her dead fish before dashing out the door. Lexi wasn't far behind her. As they raced across the street to her car, she cast a glance over her shoulder expecting to see Eric charging out but he wasn't there. As soon as they were in the vehicle, she gasped for air.

"Where the hell did you get that Taser?" Maggie asked.

"On eBay."

"Why?"

"Darlin', this is New York."

With that said, the engine roared to life, and they tore away, leaving behind Maggie's asshole ex and an apartment that would probably be torn apart by the time she got back — if she ever went back. She couldn't even imagine how bad things would get.

# Chapter 3

"You're fired!" the words echoed in Jesse's ear. He couldn't believe Alfonzo had the nerve to wait until he'd finished the last delivery before he told him.

"First off, you can't fire me, as I don't work for you."

"I pay you."

"Yeah and you owe me."

"Owe you what?"

"Eighty bucks. Forty from the first delivery, and forty from the last."

"You cost me a lot more than that today. You're lucky I'm not sending you a bill."

Jesse screamed into his phone. "You bastard. I needed that money."

"And my customers needed their packages, so I guess we're even."

"That wasn't my fault."

"See you around, Jesse."

Jesse was about to reply when the line went dead. He squeezed the phone tight and for a second he wanted to toss it over the heads of the smiling faces of those gathered in Times Square. He was fuming. Not only had a car nearly run into him, he'd been held up at gunpoint, got a flat tire on the last leg of his journey to deliver a package that he wouldn't get paid for, now he had to deal with this shit? Street Kings had been the only service that had provided him with enough steady work to pay his landlord, the rest was chump change. What was he supposed to do now? A light snow began to fall only adding to his frustration. The noise in the city was deafening. Everyone looked frozen as they eagerly waited for some dumb ass ball to drop so they could blow their horns, kiss and pretend like the next year of their lives wasn't going to be as shitty as the one they were leaving behind. The fact was for most people it wasn't getting any better. He gazed around at the mass of idiots crammed into steel pens wearing purple hats and 2019 glasses. What a bunch of morons! Police herded the crowd into spots like cattle. They weren't taking any chances. National Guard soldiers, bomb-sniffing dogs and radiation detectors were among the crowd. If that wasn't enough, thousands of protesters had gathered to vent their anger over the president's aggressive rhetoric toward North Korea, with some holding up signs that said: WE WON'T FIGHT ANOTHER RICH MAN'S WAR! and STOP THE ARGUMENTS NOW BEFORE WAR STARTS!

It was a complete circus. Jesse stared down at his phone to calculate how much he'd made for the day. When the figure came up, he groaned. He should have netted at least a hundred and forty, instead he'd barely made thirty bucks.

While he was staring at his phone, he felt a crowd of people push up against him forcing him forward into the rest of the masses. He tried to use his bike and elbows to make his way through, but it was useless, there were just too many damn people.

"Get out of the way!" he yelled but was caught among

protesters and those eager to see the ball drop. He felt like a fish trying to swim upstream. A heavy police presence moved in on the group as voices got louder, and someone fired a flare. A trail of smoke cut through the night over neon signs before a golden-orange light lit up the evening sky. The chants of protesters only incited the police. Soon what had been organized chaos turned into disorder as a line of police pushed through the crowd and started dragging people out. Jesse fell back as people landed on top of him.

"Hey!" he yelled but his voice was lost as tempers flared and protesters fought back. After managing to get to his feet he tried to escape but soon found himself caught in the middle, nothing more than another face in a crowd of protesters. A meaty hand clamped onto the back of his collar then yanked him through the crowd. His natural instincts were to pry himself loose, and he kicked back but that only added fuel to the fire. Two cops grabbed him to help their comrade and before he knew it, he was zip tied and was being thrown into the back of a police paddy wagon.

"What did I do? C'mon!"

They didn't listen but just slammed the door shut.

He didn't think his day could get any worse — how wrong he was.

* * *

Inside the police wagon, Elliot nursed a busted-up nose by turning his head and rubbing the blood off on his sleeve. He cast a glance at the new addition to the group; a young guy, mid-twenties, five foot nine, short dark spiky hair, wearing black bicycle gear, neoprene and a backpack. He shouted a few obscenities at the cop and told him he didn't have anything to do with the protest, and that they had got it all wrong.

"You're wasting your time," Elliot said as the cop told him to shut up.

The guy looked at him for a second before kicking the door. A few shards of light from neon signs filtered in through the slats in the rear. Beyond the steel the sound of the crowd raging against the system continued. Bodies slammed up against the side of the wagon making them rock inside.

"You'll only incite them further."

"Are you are a protester?" the man asked.

He shook his head. "Nope."

"The name's Jesse, you?"

"Elliot."

Jesse leaned back resigned to his fate. "So how did you wind up here?"

"They didn't have enough room in the next van. Told me I was breaking a law by rooting through the garbage searching for cans. But that's bullshit."

"Actually, it's not. Once the garbage hits the curb, legally it belongs to the city."

"What are you, sanitation police?" Elliot asked.

The guy shook his head and smiled.

Elliot continued. "Anyway, they must have thought I was some terrorist threat. They were stopping pizza guys from going into the crowd, they confiscated an umbrella from one woman and yanked one guy out for wearing a backpack."

Jesse looked at Elliot, scanning him the way others did when they tried to make sense of why he was wearing a clergyman's black outfit beneath his dirty jacket. There was no reason. He'd found it in a dumpster.

"You?" Elliot asked.

"Wrong place, wrong time."

"Story of my life," a female voice replied from farther back in the darkness of the wagon. When Elliot had been thrown in, there were already three other people inside. After fleeing his abode below Grand Central Station he'd joined the flow of pedestrians heading towards Times Square. He figured he'd be able to gather more cans in an hour there than he could on a regular day. People had nothing else to do than eat and drink while they waited. Times Square was an absolute gold mine for trash after the event, and it was even better if he got there before city sanitation workers showed up.

* * *

Jesse observed the disheveled individual. By any

measure he looked like a homeless priest. He was wearing the black outfit with the white collar but that was about where the resemblance ended. His jeans were torn and dirty, and he smelled like a dumpster.

He had a thick head of dark hair, a granite jaw and piercing dark eyes.

"Sounds like it's getting worse out there," Jesse said as the crowd's yelling got louder. He turned his attention to the others inside. Three of them were dressed in protester T-shirts. The female with dark shoulder-length hair had the word *PEACE* on the front of hers. She covered it up with her thick winter jacket.

"The cops do that?" Jesse asked gesturing to the cut on her head.

"No, that was courtesy of my ex."

"Oh," he muttered before turning away for a second then looking back at her. "I'm Jesse by the way."

"I heard you," she replied.

"And you are?"

"Not really in the mood for conversation," she said

staring down at her flat boots. She was a good-looking woman, early twenties, green eyes, and from what he could tell athletic in appearance.

A pause then she looked at him. "Sorry, the name's Maggie."

He scanned the faces of the other two across from her.

"You know each other?" Jesse asked. They shook their heads.

"No, my good friend did a runner when things got out of control."

"Left you behind?"

She pursed her lips. "Yep! Seems that way."

"So, you were here to protest?"

"No, I was here to support my friend. She said it was a surprise. Oh, it was a surprise, alright." She shook her head again looking deflated before locking her gaze on him. "I thought we were going out to celebrate the New Year. A few drinks, she said, a bite to eat and then ring in the New Year. Then once we were in the thick of the crowd, she hands me this T-shirt. Tells me that it matters.

That she'd supported me through everything I've gone through." She sighed. "What was I meant to do? I should have just stayed at home but oh, right, there is no home as probably by now my asshole ex has renovated it with his fist. I'll probably find my flat-screen in pieces, my mattress on the sidewalk and my wardrobe torn to shreds when I get back. If I get back," she added.

Jesse nodded. "And I thought I was having a bad day."

Right then the door swung open, and another man was shoved inside, he however wasn't ready to accept his fate. He used both of his feet to push back against the van and he launched himself backwards bringing down two police officers. A big mistake. Three more officers jumped into the thick of it and started beating him with their batons before he was tossed head first inside. He landed in the center of the wagon, right on top of everyone's feet. Before the door slammed, Jesse caught sight of the riot taking place outside. The cops had their hands full. Thousands were causing them no end of trouble.

The stranger coughed and then groaned.

"A little help," he muttered.

"I'd give you a hand but... I'm kinda tied up," Jesse said trying to make light of the moment as the guy struggled to get to his knees with his wrists bound together. Once he managed to slide onto a seat across from Jesse, he got a better look at him. He was a little over six foot, had a full beard, ocean blue eyes and his hair was pulled back into a man bun. He was almost the spitting image of actor Jason Momoa. Jesse even wanted to ask him if he was related but decided that would come across a little weird.

* * *

He eyed the others inside the enclosure. Damon was beyond furious at himself. He'd only been out of the clanger sixteen hours and he was already on his way back there. The parole officer wouldn't take too kindly to this. But he had no one else to blame but himself. Well he could blame Cole because if he had been there to pick him up none of this would have happened. One minute he was among the crowd breathing in freedom and relishing the sight of thousands of people just waiting to be pickpocketed, the next he was engaged in a brawl. It was not like he was trying to be greedy — he just needed about sixty bucks, enough to pay for a trip north of the city, some food and a pack of smokes. He had no trouble sliding his hand into his first victim's bag, she was so preoccupied with taking selfies, and everyone was brushing up against each other, that she didn't even feel her handbag become light. Problem was, there was only ten bucks inside. With cops everywhere, it was hard to go unnoticed. They'd been eyeing him from the moment he arrived. Probably because he wasn't wearing a New Year's Eve hat, or looking like he was with anyone. It also didn't help that a friend of the next guy whose wallet he was lifting saw everything. Before he knew it, he was in a brawl in the middle of Times Square, then being dragged out by four police officers as several people cried thief. He sighed, then cast a glance at the guy beside him who stunk to high heaven.

"So what did you do to get in here?" the guy in the

bicycle outfit asked.

"Stabbed someone in the face," he said without hesitation. It was a lie, but he didn't think it mattered. An hour from now he'd be locked up and staring down another jail sentence and the last thing he wanted to do was get friendly with anyone. Instead, he sat back, closed his eyes and thought about what had landed him the original sentence.

Contrary to what others might have thought, a year ago he had a clean record. The worst he had was a ticket for speeding. His biggest problem was hanging out with the wrong crowd. He'd taken a job as a mechanic in Keene, in upstate New York, and his co-worker and closest friend Cole had wanted him to head down to the Big Apple to collect some parts they needed because they were very large and the shipping costs were too much. He did the run, not knowing what was stored inside the engine parts. Unknown to him and Cole, the cops had been monitoring the cocaine business operating out of Brooklyn for several weeks. They waited until he had everything loaded and had driven a mile down the road before they closed in on him. Of course, he wouldn't throw Cole under the bus, so he just told the cops he didn't know about the drugs. He got eight months inside, but in Rikers that was like doing five years in a maximum prison. Every day was a test to stay alive. If he didn't have to watch his back from other inmates, it was the guards he had to worry about. Many had been charged with beating handcuffed inmates then filing false reports to cover up the attacks. It was only one of the many incidents of abuse, corruption and violence that plagued the jail.

* * *

Jesse shimmied up to the crack at the back of the wagon and tried to peer out to find out what was going on. The van was full but by the looks of it so were the hands of police officers who were still manhandling protesters.

"What can you see?" Elliot asked.

"Just a lot of…"

Then something strange happened. All the neon signs,

street lamps and hotel lights that brightly lit up the city suddenly went off. They didn't flicker, there was no delay in one over the other. One second they were on and the next they were off.

"What the?"

"What is it?" Damon asked.

Because of all the commotion in the crowd, it took curious onlookers and police a few seconds to clue into the fact that the entire city was now blanketed in darkness. Not a single light from a cell phone or an office building was on. Jesse watched as cops spoke into their radios but appeared to be getting no response. The few police vans that had been pulling away only seconds earlier had glided to a standstill as if the driver had shut off the engine. Silence swept across the crowd as if people were waiting for someone to plug the switch back in at the main power source, but nothing happened. He glanced up at the towering hotels and skyscrapers through the thin slats while Elliot badgered him to tell him what was going on.

That's when he saw it.

He took a few steps back and his eyes widened in horror.

Then the roar of the engines grew louder.

"What is it?" Maggie asked.

"A plane. There's a plane heading straight for the crowd!"

Before he could spit another word, he stumbled over Elliot's boot and landed on his back. What came next was a mixture of screams, the echo of metal hitting concrete and a gust of wind so powerful it sent the stationary wagon into a roll.

## Chapter 4

Darkness dominated. The taste of blood filled his mouth. For a brief moment Jesse thought he had died and had woken up in hell. He saw flames before him, and heard nothing but screams as the world came rushing in, getting louder and louder by the second. He was disoriented, upside down, crushed up against metal by someone else's body. In between a pair of legs, he saw fragments of the world. Slowly but surely his memories came flooding back in.

Deliveries.

Times Square.

Being arrested.

Seeing the lights go out.

And silence covering everything.

Then the plane. The sight of it sweeping down at an angle heading towards the million people crammed into the square.

He groaned and pushed his way out from underneath a limp arm and emerged crawling over the top of others who were out cold. Were they dead? At some point the doors on the back of the paddy wagon had burst open. One door was wide and providing him with a clear shot of the carnage. For as far as he could see there was blood, fire, and bodies laying everywhere. People were screaming. Police were frantically trying to help those who'd survived. It was pure torture listening to the cries. A father holding his young child in his arms, a mother or sister clinging to the hand of a dead woman and EMTs providing medical attention to others. How many had survived?

Jesse turned his attention to the others inside; he noticed his wrists were no longer bound. The plastic zip tie was still attached to one wrist but the other end was dangling. He rubbed his wrists and felt his head. It was bleeding. His first instinct was to climb out, get away before the cops could shove him back inside, but one glance outside and it was clear that the few that had survived were too busy helping the injured. He scrambled over the lifeless bodies and made his way to the door. The truck was on its side. He was about to slip out when he heard a groan behind him. Jesse turned back and sighed. He couldn't just leave them here. He had enough guilt to bear with the death of Chloe; he didn't want their lives on his conscience.

Stepping back inside he carefully made his way over to the woman he'd briefly been talking with. What was her name? Magda? Maggie. That was it.

"Maggie. Are you hurt?"

His eyes scanned her body, but it was hard to see in the darkness.

"I don't know. My leg is in a lot of pain."

She had it jammed under someone else so that might have been why. It was one of the protesters. He hadn't got the guy's name and by the looks of it he wasn't breathing. He placed two fingers on the guy's neck and that confirmed it. Perhaps he broke his neck in the tumble? Jesse rolled the guy off Maggie and helped her out of the mass of bodies. The moment he shifted her, there was another groan, then a third. He shifted Maggie into a different position before moving across to where Elliot was lying. He was face down and as he rolled him over he was now sporting a gnarly gash on the side of his face.

"Elliot. Hey!" He snapped his fingers in front of his face hoping to get his attention.

Elliot's eyelids fluttered then he stared back at him. "What happened?"

"A plane came down. The truck rolled."

"A terrorist attack?"

He shrugged. "I don't know." Jesse paused. "Can you move?"

Elliot straightened up. He wiped drool from the corner of his mouth before nodding. Seeing that he was okay, Jesse turned his attention to the next guy whose finger looked as if it was broken. It was pointing oddly. He grimaced at the sight and placed his hand on his shoulder. The man twisted over, gasping for air, completely startled.

"It's okay," he said, then repeated himself. "We need to get out of here. The truck is on fire, it might explode." Jesse looped his arm around the man's huge waist and assisted him in getting up. He pointed at his hand. "It doesn't look good."

His ring finger was bent upwards. Without hesitation the man gripped it and snapped it back into place while letting out a howl.

Jesse's eyes widened. "Holy shit."

He'd never seen anyone do that.

"What's your name?"

"Damon."

"Well Damon. Are your legs working?"

He gazed down at them and moved them. "Think so."

"Good."

Satisfied, he turned his attention to the woman who had been across from Maggie. One glance and it was easy to tell that she hadn't made it. A shard of metal was sticking through her chest and out her back. A portion of the metal grill that separated the front from the back had come loose as the truck rolled. It had twisted and cut deep into her. Jesse ran his hand over her eyelids to close them.

Everything about what was happening brought back the memories of losing Chloe. They'd known each other since college. Back then he had his eyes set on making his mark in the city. Against their parents' wishes they'd moved in together and any time the topic of marriage came up he changed it. It wasn't that he didn't want to marry her as she was everything to him. The problem was too many couples went into marriage with good intentions and ended up getting divorced and he wasn't ready to become a statistic. In many ways it seemed like a curse to him. Still, as time went by and they both ended up in secure jobs in the city, Chloe began talking about it again. *We should get married. We've been together for four years. I want to have kids.* Her biological clock was ticking and by that point he'd even warmed up to the idea of it. Now as he looked back, he wondered if that had been the reason why it had happened. Was it a curse? They'd only been married a couple of months when the accident occurred. They'd been driving back from her mother's in Jersey in late January and there was a lot of snow on the ground from what he could remember. He thought that had played a role, but the police said it hadn't, and that the other driver had been drinking, but he couldn't help think that had they seen it in time, that maybe, just maybe the outcome might have been different. It didn't help that a few weeks before that he'd given her all these reasons why they didn't need snow tires on the ground, and how all-seasons did the job if people drove slowly.

*"My parents never once put them on their vehicles and they were fine. It's all about how you drive the vehicle."*

*"And what about others?"*

*"Keep your eyes peeled."*

*"I just think paying the extra eight hundred bucks would be worth it. Peace of mind and whatnot. Besides, once the baby is here…"*

*"Baby? Are you pregnant?"*

*She laughed. "No. But we're gonna have kids, right? Once we do, I want snow tires on this car and I don't care what your parents did."*

*"I'd be driving, anyway."*

*"Jesse."*

*"Okay. Okay. I'll make a few calls when we get home."*

It had been quiet that night. Just the steady hum of the traffic on the road. It shouldn't have happened. He'd spent many a night thinking back. Chewing it over. What if he'd been driving? Would he have seen it? What if he hadn't told her that joke that caused her to take her eyes off the road for a few seconds? What if, what if…? Even after all this time the what-ifs hadn't gone away.

Twenty minutes later, somewhere on Ninth Street in Brooklyn, a truck came out of nowhere and slammed into the side, T-boning their vehicle and sending it into a spin. It collided with a streetlight, set off the airbags and shattered all the windows. By the time Jesse came to, firefighters were using the jaws of life to get both of them out. For forty minutes inside that car he had to stare at Chloe's dead face. The only thing he could do was reach over and close her eyelids.

"Jesse!" A voice from behind him snapped him out of the past. Elliot came up from behind him and placed a hand on his shoulder. "She's gone. Let's go."

He kept a firm grip on Jesse's jacket as each of them crawled out of that paddy wagon. They'd only been out a few seconds when Damon begun rubbing the plastic ties around his wrists up against the wheel well to snap the plastic. Once he was free, Maggie followed suit. There was no fear of a cop stopping them as all eyes were on the charred remains of a 747. Seats from inside were scattered, some still held dead passengers. Fire flickered into the night, casting ghostly shadows off the crumbled walls of buildings, which had been destroyed by the plane's huge engines. The entire plane had clipped buildings, shearing off large sections of concrete and bringing it down to crush those beneath. Glass lay scattered everywhere. For several minutes all four of them stood there staring into a huge gouge in the ground where the plane's nose had torn up the asphalt. It had twisted and somersaulted, spilling fuel everywhere. Chunks of rock, furniture from stores and bodies soaked in airline fuel crackled as fire consumed them. None of them had seen anything like this. The loss of lives had to have been in the thousands.

"We should help people," Maggie said, stepping over a section of the ground that had been turned up like the corner of a book.

She stumbled and Jesse stepped in to steady her. "You've taken a nasty knock to the head. I don't think you're in any state to help anyone," Jesse said. "You should probably head home. Where do you live?"

"Brooklyn," she replied.

"Huh, that's where I am," Jesse said.

Jesse caught Elliot staring up at all the buildings. For as far as the eye could see, none of the buildings had lights. The power in the entire city had gone out.

"You think it's terrorists?" Damon asked.

"Well if it is, they've managed to take out the power," Elliot replied. He trudged on, heading over to a police officer who was trying to help a woman out of a car.

"Elliot, what are you doing?"

"Finding out what's happened."

"I think it's pretty clear."

Elliot ignored him and continued to walk without any thought to the fact that the cop might try to arrest him. There was little fear of that happening. The surrounding chaos consumed the attention of emergency services. They watched as he spoke with the officer whose face was blackened by smoke. Jesse couldn't hear what they were saying, but he was nodding when he turned back.

When he returned, he wiped some blood off his face with the back of his sleeve.

"So?" Jesse asked.

"She has no idea. They heard nothing. But I have a gut feeling I know."

Elliot walked past them and Jesse grabbed him by the arm. "What?"

"Well there are only two things that can take out the power, stop cars and make planes fall out of the sky. Either a solar flare or a nuke. And with all the shit that's been happening in the news my money is on a nuke."

"A nuclear bomb?"

"An EMP. Electromagnetic pulse."

"You want to clarify?"

He sighed. "Imagine for a minute a nuclear bomb is detonated two hundred miles somewhere above the United States. It has the power to fry anything that relies on electricity. Computers, phones, newer vehicles that rely on computer circuitry. Look around you. Can you hear anything besides people crying? No sirens. No vehicles operating. That's why that plane dropped out of the sky. That's why all these lights are off in the buildings, and why none of these survivors are on phones calling home. Nothing works. It's thrown us back into the 1800s."

He shrugged Jesse's hand away and walked a short distance. Jesse stood there trying to process it all. His life had been hard enough as it was but what now? He turned and jogged over to where Elliot was.

"Okay, so the power will come back on, right? I mean.

Maybe not immediately but in a day or so, yeah?"

He scoffed. "Maybe. Maybe not. I wouldn't bank on it."

Damon looked at the carnage around them as he walked over. "For someone who looks and smells like he lives on the streets, you sure know a lot about this. How come?"

He didn't hesitate in responding. "I was in the military. We were taught about it."

"How to survive it?"

"Something like that," he said walking over to a dead body and beginning to root through the person's pockets.

"What the hell are you doing?" Maggie asked.

"Seeing if there is anything useful."

Maggie hobbled over. "Have some respect for the dead."

"I do. I'm going to use whatever he might have to stay alive. I'd recommend you do the same."

"Are you joking?"

"No, and you better get with the program quick

because if this was a nuke or solar flare, things are only going to get worse."

"Program? What are you on about? The lights have gone out, a plane has crashed, we should be helping, not stealing."

"You do whatever you have to do."

He moved on to the next person and continued rooting through pockets. Jesse scanned the area looking at those that were on the ground but still moving. He knew first aid, but it had been a while since he'd gone through any of it. While he thought about getting out of there because he had no idea what danger they were in, how could he leave these people? The police were overwhelmed. Many of them were dead themselves. The plane had literally cut through people like a hot knife through butter. They didn't stand a chance. There was nowhere they could go. Some of them had been trampled underfoot but most had been swept away by the plane, crushed or decapitated. The arm of a young child came into his line of sight and he felt his stomach lurch. Jesse had never been in a war but he imagined that the battlefield must look and sound a lot like this. Through the thick black smoke that drifted over the bodies of the living and dead, he spotted a woman whose pant legs were covered in blood. He hurried over and stooped down to check on her.

"Ma'am."

Without hesitation, she pointed off into a crowd of people.

"Please. My daughter."

He cast a glance over his shoulder.

"What does she look like?"

"Blonde, wearing a pink jacket."

"What's her name?"

"Hailey."

Jesse double-timed it over to a mass of bodies that were stacked up on top of each other, as if the wing of the plane had scooped over the top of them and blown them over. A quick glance at the surrounding area, and it was clear that wasn't what had happened. A portion of the plane had collided with the masses. Those on top were either decapitated or knocked unconscious, those below them wouldn't have been able to escape. The pure weight of bodies pressing down might have killed people.

"Hailey!" Jesse called out the kid's name, his eyes frantically searching. As he squeezed into a gap, Damon came up behind him.

"I'll check around the other side."

Over the next five minutes they called out her name without any luck and then Damon spotted her jacket. "There she is." Jesse went around to give him a hand to drag her out. From the moment they got a look at her face they could tell she was gone. Her skin had turned a light shade of blue. She'd been crushed beneath the weight of people. Jesse stared at her for a second before Damon placed his hand on his shoulder.

"I'll let her know."

He nodded as Damon returned to tell the lady. Her cries cut into the night, and that's when he knew that the situation was far bigger than they could handle. Even if they could drag people out, or manage to perform CPR on them. What then? There were no ambulances, at least none he could see. Maybe farther down? Still, there was no one that could rush away the seriously injured, and he wasn't a doctor. Self-preservation began to kick in. The thought of what might have caused this and whether there were any further threats.

## Chapter 5

On the outskirts of Lake Placid, Rayna Wilson had been in the middle of tucking her daughter Lily in for the night when all the lights went out in the house.

"Mom?"

"It's okay, it will probably come back on in a minute."

She remained beside her daughter's bed and tucked a strand of dark hair behind her ear. Lily laid back in her bed but looked worried. Ever since their father had left, her kids had changed, become more clingy, worried and scared of the darkness. The door creaked open and Evan walked in holding a blanket around him, and a flashlight in his hand.

"You think I can sleep in here tonight?"

"Of course you can."

"Mom?" Lily protested.

"It's just for the night."

"And then the next. You know how he is."

"Lily, just go to sleep."

Rayna got up and gave Evan a nod before she went into his room and dragged his mattress into her room. She dropped it on the floor beside Lily's bed and returned to grab a few more blankets. Once he had everything he needed, she told them to go to sleep.

"You not sleeping in here tonight?"

"I think you two are big enough you don't need me anymore."

She smiled, reached down and picked up Evan's flashlight.

"I need that," he said.

"So do I. I'll bring it back, okay?"

He nodded and leaned back on his pillow. She closed the door behind them and headed to check the garage for another flashlight. Before heading in she flicked the light switch on and off just to be sure that it wasn't a fuse that had blown and then she went and checked the breaker box. This had always been Elliot's job when he was around. However, she'd learned how to run the house without him while he was on deployment in Fallujah, Iraq. Stumbling around inside the garage she located the second flashlight and switched it on to make sure it was working. A large beam lit up the inside of the two-car garage. The house was too big now that he was gone. It had been a year since he'd walked out and left them behind. Even though she'd seen the writing on the wall months before that, she didn't think he would do it. In many ways she blamed the military. She'd attended the Yellow Ribbon ceremonies and listened to the information which educated spouses on deployment and what to expect when they returned home. She only wished they had provided more information on PTSD. After he had been away for an entire year, she was ecstatic to get him home. There would be no more stress, no more single parenting the kids, no more communicating over the internet and well sex, that was just the cherry on the top. At no point had she worried about how much he'd changed.

Rayna used the flashlight to search for a box of candles

and then made her way back into the three-bedroom cottage. She glanced down at his boots that were still where he'd left them after the last time he'd been in the yard. She stopped by his jacket and smelled it just so that she wouldn't feel so alone. As she went about lighting candles and placing them around the house, she thought back to the first few weeks after he got home. She noticed the small things but just notched them up to him trying to readjust to life after being overseas. As the months went by, she began to notice that he was sleepwalking more, his mood would be fine one minute and terrible the next. Then there were the sudden outbursts, avoiding others, anger over the smallest thing going wrong and freaking out when he heard a loud noise. These were just a few of the many things she'd noticed.

Soon the waters in their relationship became rocky as arguments started, and then he lashed out a few times. Not at her but at the wall, leaving huge gaping holes in the drywall. Arguments led to distance between them and before long it felt like she had a stranger in her home.

Rayna lit a candle, and it illuminated a photograph of the two of them from better days — a few years after they'd got married. Life was so different then.

After returning from deployment it all changed.

She remembered him jumping from his bed with his gun in hand and the one time he fired it above Evan's head. As hard as it was to get through that, that still wasn't the worst of it. Rayna had suggested he get help, and he did. For a short time he reached out to Veterans Affairs, and they offered help and treatment options for post-traumatic stress disorder, that's what they were calling it. Apparently, it was common in those who returned. Out of every hundred veterans, eleven to twenty suffered with it. But even with all that information and help available, it was still a struggle. There were days when he appeared to do a 360-degree turnaround and life seemed fine. There were moments when she thought it was just a matter of time, and that eventually it would pass, but inwardly she knew it wasn't going to go back to the way things were. She tried to get him to open up, and tell her about what had happened over there, but he wouldn't talk about it. She assumed he'd seen the worst of it being a combat medic, and that eventually he would come around, but the reality was, for all her pushing to try and get him help it had only made it harder.

She stared at the photo and picked it up. God, she missed him. Not the man who returned from war or the one that walked out the door on her, but him, the guy before deployment. She'd chided herself on numerous occasions for not trying hard enough, usually when the kids got home from school and needed help with their homework. That had always been Elliot's thing. He'd been a whiz at helping them while she took care of the home and made sure all their doctor appointments and after-school activities were arranged. She wished now that she'd told him that whatever had happened over there, it didn't change how she felt about him. She would still love him and was there whenever he needed to talk. Instead she had pressured him to talk about it and even blamed him when he refused to speak. She placed the photo frame back down. How did she expect him to react?

She turned to reach for her phone, instincts kicking in to call Gary Westin, a police officer and a good friend of Elliot's. Gary and his wife, Jill, had been lifesavers after Elliot had left. She'd even come to realize that Elliot's leaving wasn't uncommon in the world of PTSD. Jill was a veteran's wife, and she'd gone through it with Gary, but they'd weathered the storm together. Before joining the police, he'd done eight years in the Marines. After he returned, it had been almost every other day he would say he was leaving and that he'd be back for the rest of his stuff. Jill was full of advice, but it was a little too late.

She glanced at the phone, pressed the button but it was dead.

What on earth was going on? It was a little after nine.

She went over to the window and glanced out. The neighbor's home across the street was dark. Rayna contemplated ducking out and driving over to Jill's. They lived a fair distance from them but she didn't want to leave the kids alone. Even though Lily was fourteen now, and Evan thirteen, losing their father had made them shrink back into their shells. They were much more fearful than they had been before. Of course, in the day they acted as though none of it got to them, but nighttimes were different.

"Why can't you just go get him?" Lily would ask.

"And I miss him, Mom," Evan said often.

Neither of them fully understood what had taken place or what had led up to the incident on the night he left. Only a few knew. Moving away from the window she went back into the garage to check the breaker again. She shone the light inside the metal cupboard and flipped the switched a few times. Everything looked okay. There was no burnt smell and no wires hanging loose. Rayna went back inside and slipped on her coat, she unlocked the front door and was careful to close it quietly behind her before she jogged down the small driveway to the edge of Mirror Lake Drive. She squinted down the tree-lined road towards the home of the Thompsons. It was tucked just back from the road but she could usually see their living room through the branches and bushes. Their lights were out too. Rayna frowned. There were no vehicles on the road either. Strange. She headed back to her home and locked up as soon as she was inside. It wasn't the first time the power had gone out. The longest had been two hours after a vehicle had crashed into a transformer pole down the road, but even then she remembered her cell phone working. She stood there in the hallway of her home for a few minutes contemplating what to do before turning in for the night. It wasn't like she had plans to see in the New Year with anyone. Gary and Jill had invited her over to their place but she declined.

* * *

Fourteen miles away in the small town of Keene, just southeast of Lake Placid, Cole Tucker was sitting around a card table in the back of his auto repair garage with his pals when the lights went out. He'd planned on seeing in the New Year with a lot of drinking, drugs, sex and a few laughs with Devin, Sawyer, Magnus and Tyron. He'd wrapped up the previous day's work with every intention of going and picking up Damon in the early hours of the morning, but one thing had led to another, and after a new batch of coke had come in, he'd ended up overindulging and losing track of the time. When he awoke on New Year's Eve it was almost midday, certainly far too late to pick up Damon. He'd checked his messages and found three from him. He figured he would make his own way home. Sure, he'd be pissed but what was he supposed to do? There was no point phoning him as he'd called from a phone booth and he didn't have a cell, and even if he did, that would have only ended in an argument.

Sitting in total darkness, he waited for a few seconds thinking it was just a glitch.

"Damn it! What the hell?" He got up holding his cards. He wobbled a little, feeling intoxicated by the last three beers. "Don't touch the money. I'll go check the fuse box."

"Cole, you did give those ladies the right address, didn't you?" Magnus asked oblivious to the fact that they were now dealing with a blackout.

"You think I'm stupid?"

"No, it's just they were supposed to be here by now."

"Perhaps they got stuck in traffic," Tyron said.

"In a town with less than a thousand people? Doubt it. Idiot!"

"Hey, I'm just saying. It's New Year's Eve. People want to celebrate."

"People don't do shit in this town," Devin added.

"Ain't that the truth," Sawyer muttered tossing his cards down.

Cole kept a good eye on his cash as he checked out the fuse box at the back of the garage. He didn't trust his buddies at the best of times but after they had a few brews in them, and had been snorting the good stuff, they wouldn't think twice about swiping a couple hundred.

He fished around in a cupboard for a wind-up flashlight and gave it about twenty turns. Light filled the end of the garage revealing three vehicles they'd been working on. After seeing that everything was okay in the fuse box, he turned back to the rest. All of them were employed by him. It was a legit business but with their drug business doing well, they were picky about whose vehicles they worked on. He did just enough to keep the cops from sniffing around his place. Five years of bringing in coke from New York City, he'd never once been caught. The closest he'd come was a year ago when he'd gone with a new supplier and hadn't vetted him. He had no idea that the cops had their eyes on him until it was too late. Of course Damon wouldn't see it that way. He thought Cole had set him up and since he'd gone away, Cole had been counting down the days to his release, figuring that he would retaliate in some way. In all honesty he thought he would have ratted on him when he was caught but he didn't. That was why he'd promised him a ride that morning. He thought the drive back would give them time to chat, so he could smooth out things. Him and Damon went way back. Long before the drugs, they'd been close friends. They'd grown up together and were almost like brothers. Both of their parents had divorced, and they found solace in the company of each other, going on long bike rides through the region. Years on, it just made sense they'd work together. While the other guys had been gung-ho about earning extra money by selling drugs, Damon didn't want anything to do with it. He'd even threatened to quit working together if Cole didn't dial it back.

"Hey, I'm not getting any signal on my phone. Damn thing won't even turn on," Magnus said. "Sawyer, you got your phone?"

"No, it's on the blink."

"Tyron?"

"On the table," he said before leaning forward and snorting another line. Magnus scooped it up but got nothing. Cole went over to a mini-fridge and pulled out another bottle of beer. He twisted the top off and chugged a third of it down before wiping his lips on the back of his sleeve. "Sawyer, go check the house."

His chair scraped back as he got up to go and see.

"Cole, I've been thinking about Damon. After all that

happened, aren't you worried?" Tyron asked.

"No, why should I be? He never said anything to the cops."

"That you know about."

Cole leaned back against a counter that was loaded with greasy car parts. "No, I know him."

"Do you?"

"You got something to say, Tyron? Spit it out."

There was hesitation. He tossed his cards down and under the glow of the dim light he took a drag on his cigarette. "How do you know he isn't working with the cops? He was caught with a lot of coke and only got eight months. Now ask yourself, have you ever heard of someone getting eight months for that? My cousin ended up doing four years for less than a third of that. Which makes me think he worked out some kind of deal with them. For all we know, we might be under surveillance. The cops might just be waiting for the right time to bust us. Or maybe now that Damon is out they will send him in wearing a wire just so they can bring down the whole operation."

Cole scoffed. He didn't buy it. Damon wasn't like that. He wouldn't do that. He didn't mention their names at all. He'd said that he was going to sell the parts privately. They'd set it up, so the parts were not associated with their business. That way if anything did go wrong, the cops couldn't trace it back to them. He shook his head. "No. He's good."

"I hope so, for all our sakes. I'm not doing time. I wouldn't last in there."

Devin patted Tyron on the back. "Oh, I'm sure Bubba your cellmate would keep you company," he joked.

Sawyer returned and shrugged. "Seems the power is out in the whole neighborhood. None of the homes in the area have their lights on, and there are a couple of cars that have stalled further down the road."

Cole didn't reply. His thoughts were preoccupied by what Tyron had said. He just assumed that Damon wouldn't snitch on him but what if he was right, what if Damon had worked out some deal with the cops? Was that why he wanted Cole to pick him up? He figured Damon wouldn't have wanted anything to do with them after taking the fall. He took another swig of his drink. Well, he would soon find out once he showed his face again. That was if he even showed up. And if he was working for the cops, friend or no friend, he'd regret it.

## Chapter 6

Another loud explosion shook the earth, the force sent survivors scrambling for cover. Chunks of concrete from buildings rained down around them crushing many that had survived the first wave. In between the buildings, Elliot saw another downed plane just on the outskirts of Times Square. Instinctively he thought a terrorist attack as he hurried for cover. What else was he supposed to think?

A thick gust of debris from destroyed buildings carried through the streets covering everyone in a layer of white plaster, dust and grime.

He hit the ground, rolled then waited.

The sound of screams tore through the city. Only the sound of the injured screaming and the fire crackling could be heard. Black smoke, debris and dust carried on the wind like someone had shaken a bag of flour. He coughed and placed his shirt over the lower half of his face, just so he could breathe. The cries of the injured all around him reminded him of Fallujah. The noise, the sight of the dead, it was all coming back to him. He started having flashbacks, the same kind he had not long after returning home. The ones that had led him to retreat inward to try and cope — even after all this time, it remained at the forefront of his mind, tormenting him.

"Elliot!" Jesse cried out. "You okay?"

He managed to summon enough strength to lift a thumb.

He shook his head trying to force the images of the past from his mind. He ran a hand over his forehead and realized he was sweating profusely. As the dust began to clear he could see how the second plane had attempted to avoid the mass of people but had clipped a building and torn a huge hole out of it, then flipped and sliced through more structures before coming to rest and exploding. It was that explosion that shook the ground. He could see people crying for help, and those that had survived were trying to do what they could, but they were overwhelmed by the need.

Elliot managed to stand. He turned to his right and saw a man pressed up against a wall by a signpost that had twisted and landed on top of him, pinning him down. He was groaning, and one of his sneakers had come off. His face was streaked with blood. Even if he could get him out, he would probably die from blood loss or shock. His natural instincts as a combat medic were to help, but how? At least when he was in Iraq he had equipment, he had the presence of mind and the training to know what to do, but this was different. It was well over a year since he'd retreated away from his old life. He'd wanted to forget the faces of his fallen army buddies. It was one of the many reasons that had driven him from his family and into living on the streets. There he could forget, stay away from others, not harm anyone, especially his family.

He didn't even realize how long he'd been standing there until Maggie took a hold of his hand. "Elliot."

He turned to her, and she clicked her fingers in front of his face.

He'd frozen, reliving his army days and the final days with his family.

"Are you okay?"

He reached up and touched his head. "Yeah. I think."

Then just like that he was back in the present moment. All the sounds and horrors around him were just that, out there, no longer part of him. He looked down at her leg and noticed she was bleeding badly from when they'd been inside the police van and it had tipped.

"We should get you bandaged up. Here, take a seat."

He cast a glance over to where Jesse and Damon were. They were helping people as best as they could, a task that wasn't easy. They dragged a few people into nearby stores where owners had opened up to help the injured.

He ran his hands over her leg to check for any shrapnel, anything that might have embedded but there was nothing. He tore apart her jeans which were already ripped so he could get a better look at the leg.

"What did you do for a living?" Maggie asked.

"Before or after I moved to the city?"

She frowned. "You not from here?"

"Lake Placid," he replied. He got up and headed over to a store and snatched up a bottle of water from a case that an owner had stacked outside for people to take. He returned, screwed off the top and poured it over her leg and then tore off a portion of her shirt and used it to clean away the blood so he could get a better look. There appeared to be a six-inch gash just below the knee, it wasn't too deep but enough to cause her to lose a fair amount of blood.

"It hurts like hell. Is it bad?" she asked.

"You'll need some stitches but you'll live."

He removed his jacket and took off one of the many layers of shirts he had on to stay warm. He ripped the sleeve and used that to tie off the lower portion of her leg. For the first time in a long while he actually felt useful. That was why he'd wanted to be a medic in the first place. It was easy to kill, but healing others, helping them in their time of need, that was needed more than anything in a war. As he tied it off she winced.

"So you got family in the city, Maggie?"

"Just a couple of friends, that's it." She looked around. "I'm not even sure if they're alive."

There were so many dead bodies lying on the ground it would take hours, days, even weeks for emergency services to gather up the dead. With so many people crammed tightly into Times Square, it was far worse than any other disaster he'd witnessed on TV. And that was confined to a small section of New York. What about the rest of the city? Or the rest of the country?

"Probably best you head home," he said.

"I don't know if I have one to go back to."

He frowned. "What do you mean?"

She groaned and leaned back against a lamppost.

"My ex-boyfriend paid me a visit earlier this evening. He went ballistic. My friend tasered him before I left for the night."

"You left him there?"

She nodded. "He has a history of violence."

He shook his head. "Well you can't stay out here.

None of us can."

She studied him as he used some more water to clean up her leg around the wound.

"You said before or after. What did you mean? Where's home for you?"

"Home?" He snorted. "Up until this evening, below tracks 111 and 112 but not now."

There was a hesitation.

"You live on the streets?" she asked.

"You could say that."

"How do you survive?"

"I earn my living canning."

She didn't respond to that. It was usually a conversation killer. Elliot had met many well-meaning people in his time on the streets. Of course there were some that wouldn't give him the time of day, others spat at him and told him to get a job, and there were the religious ones who reached out and offered to help if he would embrace their religion. Okay, they didn't exactly put it that way, but he kinda knew what their agenda was.

They weren't out there serving soup and handing out blankets for the hell of it. Seeing that she wasn't going to continue the conversation he carried it. "So, no kids?"

"Not at my age. You?" Maggie asked.

"Two, back in Lake Placid."

Her eyes narrowed and then he wished he hadn't told her. He could already feel the guilt weighing down on his shoulders. Any second now she would ask the questions. Why are they there and you are here? Did you get divorced? When did you last see them? Why don't you speak to them? It was complicated. There was much more to it than what met the eye and only a few people, specifically veterans, would understand, and even then some wouldn't. Everyone dealt with PTSD in different ways. Some got help and were able to come back from it with the support and love of their family. Others retreated, and some ran away. He only wished it was easy.

"You should head home, make sure they're okay."

His head dropped. The thought of returning had entered his mind many times, but it was only that… a thought. There was the final argument with Rayna, the incident with her brother and Gary. It all came back to him as fresh as the day it occurred. He couldn't go back to that. He couldn't face her again, or his kids. What would he say?

"I don't have a ride even if I wanted."

There was a long pause as if she was contemplating his reply.

Then she blurted it out. "I have a vehicle."

He shook his head. "No."

"It's the least I can do for helping."

"I'm not doing anything anyone else wouldn't have done," he said turning and gesturing to Jesse and Damon, and the many others that were out there in the smoke-filled streets helping the injured. "Besides, your vehicle won't work," he said finishing up and covering her leg.

"Of course it will."

"Look around you, Maggie. Do you see anyone on their phone? Nothing is working. There is no electricity, no vehicles operating. You can't hear the hum of the city.

The world around us has gone silent except for the cries of the injured. It's an EMP. Whether it was caused by a nuke or solar flare, it doesn't matter, it's knocked out the power, at least in our neck of the woods and that means everything you know about society is going to come to a grinding halt. Transportation systems will cease, grocery stores will eventually be looted, hospitals will turn into morgues and soon enough this panic will turn into chaos as everyone realizes that the power isn't coming back on."

"No, I don't believe that. People will help each other."

"Yeah, probably, for a time. Some will. Some won't. Just because you would, it doesn't mean everyone else would. This city already had desperate people who would stab, shoot and steal if it meant they survived." He made a gesture with his head around him. "This is an opportunity for them to go on a rampage without consequences."

"But the police, the National Guard, other countries?"

"We don't know what has caused this, though I suspect it's North Korea. Who knows if they've hit other countries?"

"North Korea?"

"Look, what I'm saying is the sooner you can get home and heal up, the sooner you can start thinking about how to survive this. Right now, we have the upper hand." He paused and took a breath. "Some think that it will take one or two weeks for society to collapse but it's not the collapse I'm worried about, it's the unravel. Society has been unraveling long before those lights went out, now it's only going to pick up speed."

He stood to his feet.

"No," she said shaking her head. "This is bad but not that bad."

"Well I'm not going to stick around to find out."

"Where are you going?"

And just like that he was back in the past. The final argument with Rayna, and his one hand on the door with a duffel bag of belongings in the other. He pushed the thought from his mind and cast a glance over his shoulder.

"Jesse."

Jesse turned and raised a finger to indicate he'd be a minute. He was dealing with a young child. Elliot was quick to change the subject.

"You mentioned friends?" he asked her.

"They have a place in Brooklyn. It's where I was going to spend the night. My belongings are there."

"You think they headed back?"

"Maybe."

He assisted her to her feet, and she winced again while hobbling. "You okay to walk?"

She shook her head and stumbled a little but he caught her. "Yeah. It just hurts real bad."

"What about your parents?" he asked.

"Fourteen hundred miles away in Kansas."

His eyebrows arched.

"Yeah, they weren't too keen on me living so far away either."

Jesse finally made his way over along with Damon. "What do you want?"

"You mentioned you lived in Brooklyn, right?" Elliot asked.

"Yeah."

"You want to take her back home?"

Jesse looked at her and shrugged. "Sure. What neighborhood are you in?"

"Bushwick but my friends live in Williamsburg. That's where my stuff is. You?"

"Bed-Stuy."

Jesse turned to Elliot. "What about you?"

"I'll be fine."

They glanced at Damon and before they said anything he waved them off. "I was just on my way to the Greyhound station."

"They won't be running," Elliot said. He reached into his pocket to pull out a packet of smokes. Damon eyed the packet as he tapped one out and he got a sense he wanted one. "You smoke?"

He nodded so Elliot handed him one. He lit one and a rush of nicotine hit his system making him feel at ease if only for a few seconds.

"Are you sure you don't want to come?" Maggie asked Elliot. "I kinda feel bad leaving you here."

"We'll be fine," Elliot said. He then corrected himself. "I mean, I'll be fine."

"Where's home for you?" Jesse asked Damon.

"Keene."

Elliot blew out a plume of smoke from the corner of his mouth and squinted. "Keene, New York?"

He nodded. "You know it?"

"I'm originally from Lake Placid."

"Huh, how about that? So, what brought you down here?"

Elliot didn't want to get into it. He looked around at the devastation and although he might have been able to survive by going back underground, finding another spot and continuing to live a hand to mouth existence by looting stores, he couldn't push from his mind what Maggie had said about his kids. The only reason he was able to stay in the city was because he knew they would be safe with Rayna. She was a strong woman and more than capable of raising them by herself. He turned away from Damon and looked at the remains of the plane and chewed it over in his mind even as Damon continued to badger him with questions. Perhaps having his place set on fire was for a reason. Maybe all of this was for a reason? He couldn't stay now. Not if this was what he thought it was, but on the other hand he wasn't sure he was ready to face the music back in Lake Placid. He needed to find out more before making a decision.

"You know what, change of plans, I'll go with you. You know, just to make sure you get home safe."

"She'll be fine," Jesse reassured him.

"You know the city?" he asked.

"Like the back of my hand."

He nodded and was about to turn away when Maggie piped up. "Elliot, you're more than welcome."

He smiled, she reminded him of his own daughter.

"Just out of curiosity, what vehicle do you have?"

"An '85 station wagon. Used to belong to my father."

He grimaced figuring it might be too new.

"People still drive those?" Damon asked.

"People with little money do," she said before her mouth formed a weak, painful smile. She turned her attention back to Elliot. "Look, the offer still stands, if you can get it working. I mean, if it will work at all."

"Why?" Elliot asked.

"Why what" Maggie replied.

"Why do you want to help me?"

She looked around at all the need, then she turned back. "Maybe I can't help everyone but I can help one person."

Elliot gripped her arm and gave it a gentle squeeze. "Thank you. Let's hope it works."

Jesse got this confused look on his face. "You want to fill me in on what's going on?"

Elliot made a gesture towards the street that would lead them out of the chaos. "Society is unraveling. I'll tell you about it on the way."

## Chapter 7

Rayna tossed and turned for close to an hour before she got out of bed. She couldn't sleep, something about the outage didn't feel right. She glanced at her phone which was still getting no signal. She swung her legs off the bed and sat there for a few minutes listening to the water pipes groaning. For the past few weeks she'd been worried about them freezing up and bursting due to all the cold weather they'd had. Her mind went back to the conversations she'd had with Elliot before the last time he'd deployed. He'd walked her around the house to show her what to do in the event of a pipe bursting.

*"Shut the water off at the main shutoff valve. It's right here."*

*"Elliot. I already know this."*

*He smiled. "I know you do but I'm just testing."*

*"You and your testing," she said leaning against him. "Just make sure you come home." She raised up on her tiptoes*

*and pressed her lips against his. He pulled away, and she was going to say something but she didn't. She could tell his mind was distracted by all the things that he wanted to show her before he left. It bothered him that she was by herself even though she had a few friends in town. Lake Placid was a friendly town with just under 2,500 people though that swelled by three times in the summer months. Even the winter months still remained busy as tourists from all over the country wanted to visit the small town that had hosted the Winter Olympics back in 1980.*

*"Remember, I've put the key to the rifle cabinet in this tin." He reached up to a shelf which was out of sight and pulled out an old tobacco tin. "There is ammo in the locked drawer in my study, okay?"*

*"Yes, yes," she said smiling. "How many times have you taken me through this?"*

*"Enough but repetition is the…"*

*"… mother of all learning," she cut him off before he could finish.*

*He leaned back against the workbench. "Okay then,*

*smart ass. What about the bunker?"*

*"What about it?"*

*"What's the one rule?"*

*Her eyes squinted. "Don't tell anyone."*

*"Exactly! Okay, I think you're all good."*

Her mind flipped back to the present as she got up and picked up the flashlight off the side table and went and checked on the kids. She eased their door open and peeked inside. Both of them were out like a light. Rayna pulled the door shut and headed downstairs and entered the kitchen. Kong lifted his furry head and looked at her.

Kong was a German shepherd service dog that they'd got for Elliot six months after he returned from a deployment. For a brief while it had helped him. At least in the daytime hours but at night that was the worst. When he had the nightmares, there was nothing the dog could do for him until he woke. Ever since Elliot had left, Kong hadn't been the same. He looked as lost as Elliot did in the days leading up to the incident.

"Hey Kong, you okay, boy?"

He wagged his tail and lifted his head and she crouched down and ran a hand around the back of his ear. At least with him still here she didn't feel as nervous. Sure, Elliot had taught her how to use a rifle, but just having the dog there made her feel at peace. His tongue dangled out the side of his mouth and she looked over to his bowl and noticed he'd drunk all the water. She scooped it up and went about filling it. As she turned on the faucet, it let out a clanging sound then the water rushed out. As it filled the bowl, she thought back to what Elliot had said years ago.

*"If the lights ever go out for longer than twenty-four hours, or you find out the grid has gone down, fill up the bath and sinks with what's left of the water in the pipes as there is a good chance that's all you're going to get. You'll need it."*

As she looked out the back window, and saw no lights in the distance, her heartbeat sped up a little. There had been a number of times the power had gone out in their part of town but it had always come back up again within the hour. She glanced at her watch and noticed it had been at least two hours without power. Whether it was nerves or instinct, she wasn't sure but after placing Kong's bowl on the floor, she went back to the sink and filled it up, then went upstairs to the bathroom and did the same with the bathtub. If the grid was down, it would mean no electricity, no heating, no internet, no refrigeration, no phones and no means of withdrawing money or filling up their vehicle with gas. The vehicle? She stopped what she was doing and hurried down the stairs and scooped up the keys off the hook and headed outside to the SUV. She hit the key fob, but it didn't work. She inserted the key and then tried firing it up. Nothing. Not even a splutter. *What had he said about that?* She got out of the vehicle and headed back into the house and made her way down to the basement. Inside the laundry room at the back, she approached the workbench and opened a couple of the drawers searching for the small booklet that Elliot had created which listed what to do in the event of a crisis. He wasn't paranoid like some were and neither had he spent his weekends researching everything to do with survival, but he liked to be prepared and when the topic came up with Gary, he would just say that it was like insurance. No one wanted to use it, but it was helpful to have it. Rooting through the drawer she took out papers until she came across the small brown moleskin notebook. It wasn't full of hundreds of pages of what to do in the event the world went to shit, but there were a few pages where he'd jotted down what she and the kids were to do in the event of an… She rifled through the book and stopped… *EMP*. That's what he called it. She ran a finger down the page looking at all the signs. Sure enough, they were all there. The electrical grid would go down, GPS would no longer work, cell phones would be useless, internet, modern cars, radios and many electrical devices wouldn't work. Her heartbeat sped up as she ran a hand over the bottom of her jaw.

*"I'm telling you, Rayna, it's not as far-fetched as it might sound. We've already experienced solar storms, and with the way things are heating up with North Korea it's only a*

*matter of time before someone launches a nuke."*

It wasn't that she didn't believe him, but she didn't expect it the way he did. Perhaps it was his training in the army or his need to protect his family, but she recalled him putting into place things that might be of use. He'd started with something simple, the bug-out bag, and expanded it beyond that to creating a small storehouse of canned goods, grains, salt, water and pharmaceutical products. It wasn't a lot, just enough to see their family through six months if push came to shove. Now she was beginning to see the benefit. She continued flipping the pages and remembering what he said.

*"Come on, Elliot, don't you think you're taking things a bit too seriously?"*

*"I'm telling you, Rayna, the biggest threat facing our country right now isn't chemical warfare, climate change or even a disease, it's an electromagnetic pulse attack from a rogue nation like North Korea or Iran."*

*"But we're on the East Coast!"*

*"Doesn't matter. All it would take is one or two ballistic*

*missiles launched from a freighter or a sub in international waters and it could fry the electrical grid. Everything we have, food and water supplies, banking, medical care, law enforcement, communication and more, relies on a functioning electrical grid."*

*She studied his face and could tell he wasn't exaggerating.*

*"And if it did go down?"*

*"Some say it could kill up to 90 percent of the population in a matter of eighteen months. The fact is America is just not prepared to deal with that kind of widespread devastation. Add to that a lack of clean water, no air traffic control, no financial transactions, most would die from starvation, others from lack of hygiene and all of that without a rogue nation ever stepping foot on U.S. soil."*

*"And what about fallout?"*

*"The casualties wouldn't really be from the high-altitude explosion as it would happen too high for the nuclear effects to be felt strongly on the ground, so to speak, but it would be the domino effect that would knock everything else down." He breathed in deeply. "That's why I've put these things in*

*place because I don't know if I'll even be in the country if and when it ever occurs."*

*"Well let's hope it doesn't," she replied.*

Rayna gripped the notebook tightly and looked at the steps he'd wanted her to take if he wasn't around.

*"You'll find in the shelter a set of two-way radios. I've already given one of these to Gary. Now if I was here, we'd get in contact with family and make sure that they knew to head to the shelter. Just remember, the landlines might still work if there is an EMP. While the cell phones will be down, many of the companies now use backup generators and they might kick in and last for another week so try that first, otherwise resort to the two-way radios. But remember, Rayna, if an EMP does happen, I want you to go through the process of doing a few simple things first to see how bad it is. Look outside, check if there are any other lights on? Can you hear traffic? Test your cell phone. Try the landline. If any of those work, try and contact someone across town then out-of-state. If there is nothing and you can't communicate with anyone, then I want you to check the ham radio in the*

*shelter. Turn it on and see if there are any updates on the disaster. But just remember the EMP might have taken out stations in range, so I've left a list of different stations to tune into beside the ham radio along with how to operate it. You got that?"*

*She remembered nodding but barely processing what he was saying.*

*"Next I want you and the kids to get into the shelter. There is enough food and water down there to last for six months. The only ones who know about it are Gary and Jill. That's because I don't want you to be alone and I trust Gary. There is no telling when looters will start checking homes."*

*"And what if there is something you've forgotten?" she asked.*

*"There isn't."*

*"But what if there is?"*

*"Then you take the rifle with you and have Gary go get it. Few people are going to mess with a police officer," he said, then he turned back to the gun cabinet and clicked his fingers. "Oh, and whatever you do, don't go drinking the tap*

*water without purifying it first. Once the power goes out, the water treatment plants* aren't *going to be operating and I don't want you or the kids to end up with some disease. You'll find purifying tablets in the shelter."*

*"You honestly expect us to go down into that bunker? Why not just stay in the house?"*

*He snorted. "You're not seeing the full picture here, darling. Maybe people won't show up within 72 hours, perhaps they won't go searching homes in a week but eventually they will show up. Desperation will kick in. Starvation can drive a man to do all manner of things. Just do what I say and if you forget, refer to this book, okay?"*

*He placed it in her hands and laid his hand on top and she got a sense that he was doing this because he cared, not because he was paranoid or thought the world was going to come to an end, but because he felt it was his responsibility as a father and husband to take care of his own.*

It was for that reason alone she never argued. Even as he replenished the shelter that he'd had built into the yard not long after they'd moved in, she didn't question it.

Rayna closed the book and was about to head for the shelter when she heard a knock at the door. It was hard. Her mind went into overdrive. Who the hell was knocking at the door after eleven at night?

# Chapter 8

Without the subway or cabs in operation, they were looking at it taking them at least an hour and forty-five minutes heading south on Broadway. It was a good five-mile hike to Williamsburg from Times Square. The only reason Elliot was willing to go was the possibility that Maggie's vehicle would still be operational.

"So, run that by me again. You're saying that all vehicles won't work because the electrical is fried?" Maggie asked.

"We've never been in a situation like this before, of course, but essentially that's it. It's a bit more complicated than that, though. Newer cars today have had computers integrated into the functionality of moving parts. Obviously, manufacturers have done this to save gas, reduce breakdowns of major parts and so they can provide accessory options. The problem is that makes them vulnerable to an EMP blast. Then again, there is a lot of debate on it because some say that it depends on which way your vehicle is facing in respect to a nuclear detonation, the height of detonation, the output of the detonation, the distance and the strength of the magnetic field between the location of your vehicle and the detonation. Then on top of that you have other variables like whether your car is parked outside, inside a concrete or metal garage and so on."

Maggie had a curious mind unlike the other two who were busy gaping at the devastation around them and at survivors trying to flee the area.

"And so you think my station wagon will work because of its age?"

"You said it's a 1985 Mercedes station wagon, right?"

"Yeah."

"Well, most manufacturers didn't start placing computer chips in vehicles until the early '80s, however there were a handful of vehicles in the mid '70s that added integrated circuits. Basically, it's a bit hit and miss when it comes to these things."

"But fuel wouldn't degrade or run out for a while, will it?" Jesse asked.

"No, it wouldn't but it wouldn't take long. Think back to Katrina. Gas prices surged, the lines were horrendous, and many people were having to drive farther away to find a station that was even open. And back then there was electricity for the most part. Without electricity the gas stations aren't going to be operational. We'll be left siphoning from stalled vehicles, and that isn't always easy as the newer models have anti-siphoning in place."

Jesse turned to Damon and frowned. "Remind me again why you are coming with us?"

Damon didn't crack a smile. "If Elliot plans on using a vehicle to head back to Lake Placid, I'm hitching a ride. That's a long way to walk."

Jesse nodded and turned his attention back to the road. They were heading southwest on Broadway towards West 43rd Street. Elliot had no intention of leaving the city until this shit storm had hit, and now he was starting to question why he'd told Damon that he was heading back to Lake Placid. He didn't want to be responsible for anyone, and quite frankly he didn't know any of these people. It didn't help that Damon didn't exactly look trustworthy. His skin was covered in tattoos and he had this hard look to his face as if he'd spent years on the streets. Elliot glanced at Maggie's leg and then at Jesse. He had contemplated letting Jesse take her home by himself but without a vehicle, Damon was right, it would take them forever to get back. And he had to get back. It was one thing to leave Rayna and the kids behind when the world was functioning, another to know that they were alone while society unraveled around them. He only hoped that Rayna had remembered the notebook, or had managed to get in contact with Gary.

"So, if you're from Keene, why are you down here? Where were you before this?" Jesse asked Damon.

He glanced at him and smirked. "You've got a lot of questions."

"Just curious."

"Yeah, well maybe I don't like answering them."

He pressed on and Jesse scowled. Elliot wasn't too bothered by Damon's wish to not discuss his background. He'd met all types in his time on the streets. People ended up in New York for many reasons, and it wasn't uncommon to meet folks who were tight-lipped about those reasons. He certainly wasn't going to share his life story with the rest of them. As soon as they reached Broadway, he'd test her car out and if it fired up, he planned on taking it with or without them.

Ahead of them there were hundreds of people threading their way down the sidewalk and around stalled vehicles in the middle of the street, all of them had this deer in the headlights look on their faces. He spotted a few homeless people, those he'd met in the underground, good folks. Several people shot by on bicycles, nearly bumping into people and causing some to curse. Besides the sound of chatter as people discussed what might have caused the blackout, it was eerily quiet. The regular sounds of the city had vanished. There were no cab drivers honking their horns, no tourist buses taking people around the city, no emergency sirens, just idle chatter.

Maggie turned around and looked back towards Times Square. "It feels wrong to leave."

"There's nothing you can do," Elliot reminded her. As selfish as it might have seemed, their lives mattered as much as those who had fallen. Besides, they didn't know the full extent of what had happened, right now he was going on his gut instincts and the news he'd read about North Korea in the days prior. For all he knew, it could have just been a solar storm and maybe only New York had been affected.

"But how will these people survive if there is no emergency service?"

Elliot shrugged. He was beyond having a discussion about it. His mind was too preoccupied by his kids. It seemed almost ironic that it had taken something as drastic as this to snap him out of the mental prison PTSD had placed him in. Fortunately, Jesse was quick to fill in the void and answer her question.

"They'll have to deal with it the way they did before we had electricity, one at a time, however, I don't expect many will stick around to help, would you?"

"Of course I would. If my damn leg wasn't bleeding so much I would have stayed back there."

"Well, aren't you just the Florence Nightingale," Jesse said.

She shot him a dirty look. "It's called being human."

"Yeah, well why does it take an event like this for people to start treating each other like humans?"

"What are you on about?" Maggie asked.

"I would clarify but I can't be bothered. Not after the day I've had. I just want to get home, have a beer and wait for all this to blow over," Damon said.

"It's not going to blow over," Elliot added gazing into dark stores.

"Of course it will. It always does. Look at 9/11. New York bounced back from that. Look at Katrina, New Orleans, and all the disasters that have happened around the world. Even if the U.S. is in dire straits, other countries will offer aid. Give it a week and someone will throw the switch back on, set up a GoFundMe page and a month from now we'll be laughing at all of this."

Elliot chuckled.

"What?" Damon asked.

"Flip the switch? You think this is just about flipping a switch?" Elliot said. "Think about this, Einstein. How long did it take the government to come to the aid of those in Katrina? It was painfully slow because they had to assess, create plans and put in place the teams who would help. That relied on communication, boats, planes, cars. None of that is working right now. We are on our own! Besides, if we just experienced two downed airliners in a small section of Manhattan, think about how many are flying over North America at any given moment? You are looking at around 5,000. Sure, not all of them are going to hit heavily populated areas when they come down, but many will. Then if you think that the emergency services rely on communication, such as online, satellite and telephone infrastructure to support

320 million in the USA, and you are now dealing with one hell of a problem that won't solve itself overnight, nor will it fix itself within a week or even a month. Now consider the country's food supplies being decimated by radiation and you have one hell of a serious problem on your hands."

Damon cast a glance over his shoulder and looked as if he was about to say something but then looked away. Maggie shook her head. "No, I don't believe it."

"It doesn't matter what you believe, look around you. Only the strong are going to survive this."

"Like you?" Jesse asked.

Elliot smiled. "Look, folks like myself, and those that were spat upon by society have a chance of riding this out because we've been living in far worse conditions even when society was functioning, but the rest? Well, that's a crapshoot. Most city slickers aren't going to be prepared for this. They'll have the same mindset as you. You know, that government will have safeguards in place for events like this. That someone is going to swoop in and save the day, but I pose this question to you? What if they don't? Huh? What if you have to survive the next month or more before government restores everything? How will you manage?"

She starred back blankly.

"Exactly! The fact is most people don't know how to make a shelter, a fire, how to purify water, or what food to stock. It won't take long for people to fall sick. Pharmacies will be raided and without medicine in place, it won't take long for people to die. The truth is no one stocks up in preparation. Most don't do it. They spend thousands of dollars every year on a car, home and life insurance, they fill up their pension plans with thousands, and yet they don't think for even a second about creating a bug-out bag or having some backup plan in place for when the shit hits the fan."

"And you do?" Jesse asked. "Because forgive me for saying this but it doesn't look like you're ready. I mean you're good at lecturing but what have you got in place, Elliot?"

Elliot looked at him and shook his head. There was no point trying to explain it. He understood Jesse's frustration, but it was a little too late. "Listen, there is something I need to collect before we head over to Brooklyn. I need to duck down into the station on 28th Street. You can wait outside or come with me."

"What is it?" Maggie asked.

"Just a few things I need."

As they came around the corner that joined Broadway with 28th Street, there was a stream of people coming out of the subway station. Even as they pushed their way through, some of the ones exiting told them there was no point as it was pitch-dark down there and none of the trains were running. Elliot ignored them and elbowed his way down the steps, stopping only to take out a small LED flashlight from his pocket and switch it on. It illuminated the way as they weaved their way through the endless stream of grumbling New Yorkers. Hell, on a good day they were grumpy bastards, but this was truly bringing out the worst in them. Once they made it to the lower section and over to the platform, Elliot didn't waste a second. He hopped down onto the track without even looking. He trudged on then stopped to look back at the other three standing on the platform.

"Well, are you coming?"

"Where the hell are you going, Elliot?"

"Fine, stay here, I'll be right back."

He continued on, leaving them there while he headed further into the tunnel. It wasn't far from there. Even though he knew those that lived underground because he saw them on a regular basis, he didn't trust them so he always kept his valuables in different spots, but this was one item he hadn't returned to since arriving in New York. He hopped up onto a small concrete platform and went up a series of steps, pushed through a gate and entered a crew room. It was dark and dingy inside. A large rat scuttled across the floor out of sight. The floor was littered with dirty needles, clothes, a stained mattress and empty cans of beer and bottles of wine. He shone his light up to where all the pipes were and then put the flashlight between his teeth. He pulled himself up and carefully moved along the brake dust-covered pipes until he saw it. He reached for the backpack and pulled it out of its spot behind a piece of cardboard.

He unzipped it and shone the light inside.

Sure enough it was all still there, just as he had left it.

He'd created the bug-out bag many years ago and for the longest time it had been stored in his garage, ready for when things went wrong. His mind flipped back to that night. The night it all went wrong. The argument with Rayna. The fight with Gary and the gun going off. His stomach sank and for a second he thought about just staying in that dark room. The other three would eventually leave and he could go back to living his life away from the pain, away from the memories. He wouldn't have to face her, or him, or his kids.

The guilt was agonizing.

Elliot remained there for a few more minutes before slipping his arm under one of the straps and heading back. When he returned to the platform, he heard

Damon's voice.

"There he is."

"What the hell took you so long?" Jesse asked.

"I got lost," he replied not wishing to go into it.

"What's in that?" Maggie asked.

He contemplated showing them but that would have just raised more questions and right now he was tired of answering them. All he could think about was his kids. The longer it took him to get back, the greater the chance of them not being able to survive this, and after all he'd been through, he couldn't have that on his conscience. It would be the final nail in the coffin.

"Doesn't matter, let's get you home."

# Chapter 9

Magnus popped open another bottle of bubbly and took a hard swig on it. "So Cole, I've had some thoughts about what we should be doing this year, with the business and all. We should consider expanding into Lake Placid. The place is crawling with tourists who are looking to get loaded while on vacation."

"Don't be stupid. The reason we haven't been caught is because we only deal with those that we know. You start going into foreign territory and you're just asking for trouble."

He laughed. "I'm not saying we would go do it or that we would deal on the street. I'm talking about making some new connections. My cousin Trent is there, he's already got a small deal going on the side with some locals. It would be easy money."

"Yeah and look how that worked last time."

"Hey, that wasn't my fault. My brother had been using

that dealer for a long time and never had issues."

"Well someone did, and I'm pretty sure Damon is going to want answers when he returns."

"Ah fuck Damon. Honestly, if you had a lick of sense, you would cut ties with him now before he drags us down. I'm telling you. I don't trust him. Tyron is right, there is no way in hell he would have only got eight months inside for that stash. He's working with the cops."

"You don't know that."

He shrugged and took another swig from the oversized bottle. "Well I'm not going to wait to find out."

Cole got up and grabbed him around the throat causing him to drop the bottle. It smashed on the ground as he pushed him up against the wall. "Are you in charge, huh? You in charge of this operation?"

Magnus shook his head, a look of defiance in his eyes.

"Don't forget it and that goes for the rest of you. No one touches him, not until I have had a chance to speak with him."

"It might be too late."

Cole slapped Magnus across the face and then gripped his cheeks with one hand digging his fingers into his skin. "What did I just say? Now shut the fuck up and go find out where those escorts are." He shoved him away and Magnus gave him a dirty look before kicking a garbage can in anger and storming out.

"You know you're not doing yourself any favors, Cole," Sawyer said. "You don't want to turn Magnus against you, or any of us."

"Or what? You going to rat on me? Huh?" He jabbed his finger in front of Sawyer's face. "Damon might have worked out some deal but so far he hasn't ratted and until I know for sure what happened, no one is to touch him, do you understand?"

Sawyer pulled a face. "You're running the show, boss."

"Damn right I am."

Cole swiped up a beer and went over to the door that led into the house. He went into the kitchen and fished around inside a cupboard for his Glock. It was still in a case. He pulled it out and popped it open, then went about filling a magazine up with bullets. He wasn't stupid, and he understood where the other guys were coming from, if Damon did bring the cops with him, he would be ready. There was no way in hell he was going to do time inside. His mind drifted back to that day when him and Damon headed down to New York to make the pickup. He knew Damon was nervous about it but he didn't think there was anything to worry about. He'd gone on these runs countless times.

*"So you are staying in New York and I'm driving back?"*

*"I have to meet with a few suppliers, pay up some debt I owe. It'll be fine, you just meet this guy down at the harbor. It's all paid for. They'll load up the engine onto the back of the pickup truck and you head home. Piece of cake."*

*"You better not be screwing me over, Cole."*

*"Would I do that?"*

Cole tucked the loaded Glock into the front of his pants and gazed at a photo of him and Damon back in the day, long before they'd got wrapped up in drugs. He'd contemplated getting out of it but with all the money that it brought in, what was he supposed to do? Turn it down and go back to working a regular job? Hell no!

* * *

Rayna froze for a second. Perhaps it was just a tree branch knocking against the side of the house. She'd been meaning to cut back the branches as they'd overgrown and were brushing up against the house. Kong began barking, and she knew it wasn't any branch. She hurried up the steps to the ground floor and peered down the hallway to the door. Beyond the opaque glass she couldn't see anyone. Not even a silhouette but something was bothering Kong.

"Kong!" she said in a low voice. He turned and trotted down to her. She patted him on the head. "What did you hear, boy?" She eyed the front door and swallowed hard. That was one thing she hadn't got used to since Elliot had left. Even though the home was set up with a security system, and they had Kong and a rifle, she still felt nervous. Slowly but surely she made her way down to the door and peered out the side window. There was no one there. No vehicle in the driveway. Perhaps it was just a neighbor checking in on her? She glanced at her watch again. It was a little after midnight now. She then smiled. Oh, it was probably just folks partying and seeing in the New Year. No doubt people were out on the streets drinking and celebrating. She bit down on the side of her lip then shook her head. It was a good ten-minute drive into town, twenty-five if she walked. It had to be a neighbor. There had been a new guy move in with his brother just two homes down. Both of them looked shifty. She'd seen them slow down their truck a week ago when she was outside cleaning the SUV with Lily. She thought they were going to ask for directions but as soon as she glanced their way they took off.

She crossed the room to the wall where the security system was. It was off. No power. No security. Great. She glanced down at Kong who cocked his head to one side as if thinking that she was making a fuss out of nothing.

"I know, Kong, but we can't be too careful," she said patting him on the head before heading down to unlock the gun cabinet and retrieve the Winchester lever-action rifle. Even as she went about locating the bullets and loading it she was thinking it was foolish. There probably wasn't anything to worry about. The lights would come on soon and she'd be feeling like an idiot.

She glanced again at her watch.

*C'mon. When is this damn electricity coming back on?* she thought. It was beginning to frustrate her. After loading the gun, she scooped up a jacket and boots and prepared to go out into the backyard to collect the two-way radio and contact Gary and Jill. Her mind was whirling as she unlocked the back door, flicked on a flashlight and shone the beam across the yard. Their property was large, covering about three acres. At the far end of the yard Elliot had built a shed on top of the entrance to the underground shelter. Rayna had only been in there on two occasions; once after he had it installed, and the other was a year later when he replenished some of the stock and was planning to deploy. He'd taken her through how to access it, how to turn on the air filtration system and how to escape if a fire started.

"Come on then, Kong," she said as she ventured out. He bounded out thinking that she was going to play with him and toss his Frisbee around. She closed the door and locked it behind her, mindful that her children were inside. Outside a light rain was coming down, so she pulled up the hood on her rain jacket and kept a firm grip on the flashlight and rifle as she double-timed it across the yard.

The shed wasn't fancy, just an eight-by-twelve-foot Sunshine Shed that was used to store the lawn mower, garden tools and bags of fertilizer. Elliot had always been adamant that it had to look normal. She tucked the flashlight under her arm as she fumbled with the keys, casting a glance over her shoulder nervously. Kong was panting and sniffing around in the flowerbed nearby. After unlocking the door she entered and whistled for him to follow. Kong didn't hesitate, he bounded inside the shed and continued sniffing while she closed the door behind her. On the ground was a thick outdoor mat that was used to cover up a wooden trap door with another lock. “Kong, over here,” she said motioning for him to get behind her while she lifted the mat and unlocked it. While she was in the middle of doing it, she heard what sounded like a stick snapping outside. She froze and Kong started snarling.

“What is it, boy?”

The dog turned and pressed his nose up against the door, pulling back his gums to reveal his sharp set of teeth. She’d never seen him attack, and he wasn’t trained for that. By any measure he was a gentle dog that was meant to assist Elliot through the rough times. The key was in the lock as she lifted her head to one of the three windows.

“Don’t give away the location,” Elliot had said.

She decided not to unlock it and simply covered it up again. Her pulse sped up at the thought of having to go outside. Even though she had Kong, and the rifle, she was as nervous as hell. *Okay, Rayna, get a grip,* she told herself, trying to rein in her emotions.

Rayna pushed the shed door open and Kong slipped out disappearing into the darkness.

"Kong!" she yelled. Outside the rain was coming down even harder. She ducked out following Kong. He had crossed the yard and gone down the side of the house. The only times he'd run off and not listened to her was when there was a rabbit or another dog nearby. As she jogged around the side of the house, Kong came into view. He was standing at the front of the house barking at two strangers who had hoods over their heads. Rayna raised up her rifle, and they spotted her. One of them tossed back his hood to reveal a familiar face. It was her neighbor from two houses down and his brother.

"Whoa! Steady there, we aren't going to hurt you, we were just checking out if everyone else's power was out."

She didn't lower the rifle, but she told Kong to get back. He was barking at them and snarling.

"At midnight?"

He shrugged. "I know. It's late. We didn't mean to

scare you. I'm Austin and this is Trent, my brother."

Austin was close to six foot, bleached hair, rugged in appearance and certainly more than capable of taking down her 150-pound frame, if that was what he had in mind. Trent was darker in appearance as if he'd spent a great deal of time in a tanning booth. He had longer, dark hair that draped down to his jawline. His eyes kept bouncing between her and the house.

"I know who you are."

"So your power is out too?"

She nodded and cast up her eyes to the room that had her kids inside after seeing Trent look up. Sure enough, Lily and Evan were awake and staring.

"Just you and the kids?" Trent asked.

She didn't respond to that. Something about the question seemed real odd, especially being that it was midnight, and they had no right to come onto her property.

"I don't have anything, so you better be on your way."

Elliot had instructed her to never let up an inch. If

anyone walked onto the property, day or night and he wasn't there, not to think twice about aiming a gun at them.

Austin pumped his hands in the air.

"Okay, okay, sorry to have bothered you." Austin started backing up and kept an eye on Kong who wasn't moving an inch. She had no idea if he would attack them but she wouldn't have put it past him. Elliot told her that it was hard-wired into German shepherd dogs, and that's why they were perfect for cops and military. They would literally take a bullet if need be. Slowly the two men turned and headed out but not before Trent tossed another menacing look over his shoulder. There was something about the way he eyed her that made her blood run cold.

Once they were out of sight she whistled to Kong and they headed back inside. She'd wait until morning to contact Gary. There was no point getting all excited right now if it was just a false alarm. She chided herself inwardly as she shook the rain from her jacket and hung it up. Here she was buying into the words of a husband that had walked out over a year ago. Stupid, she muttered under her breath.

"Mom? Who were those men?"

She poked her head around the corner and at the top of the stairs Lily was standing there with Evan. They both looked frightened.

"It's okay. Go on back to bed. I'll be there in a minute."

She made a gesture with her head for Kong to go up and sit with them and off he went. She spent a couple more minutes going around to the rooms and checking that all the doors and windows were locked before heading upstairs herself.

She carried the gun with her into the bedroom and lay down beside Evan thinking about the two men and running through scenarios of what she would do if anyone ever tried to attack them. Rayna had never had problems with anyone in all the years she'd lived in Lake Placid. Overall it was a quiet town, people were friendly even though according to Gary, there was a one in twenty-two chance of becoming a victim of property crime. She'd grown up there, born and raised, and had met Elliot when she was in her college years, though they never officially got together until she took a job working at the Lake Placid Winter Olympic Museum. Unbeknownst to her when he was home on leave he'd got in contact with her parents to ask her out. He'd always been the type of person that didn't mess around. He was either all in, or out. Perhaps that's why it didn't strike her as odd when he upped and walked out on them.

Outside it was still dark, she could hear a great horned owl calling. As she started drifting off, her overly nervous mind ran rampant imagining all the worst that could happen if the power wasn't on by the morning.

It was in times like this she really wished Elliot hadn't gone.

# Chapter 10

It took close to two hours of trudging through Manhattan, and weaving their way around hundreds of stalled vehicles, before they crossed over the East River and made it into Williamsburg. Contrary to what Elliot might have believed, New Yorkers didn't appear to be unraveling. Sure, they had seen a few looters as they came past East Village but it was nothing drastic. Store owners with a lick of sense had brought down their shutters to prevent anyone from breaking in. Maggie eavesdropped on the conversations of strangers as they made their way back to Lexi's place. She figured Lexi and Matt would have headed back and were probably sloshed by now, completely unaware of the disaster that had just taken place. She even expected to find them getting it on when she knocked on the door. Lexi lived in a six-story apartment block on South Fourth Street. It was a drab-looking building with old air-conditioning units sticking out of windows, and a black fire escape that snaked its way up the brown brick structure.

Relieved to have made it in one piece, she shouldered the front door, but it was locked. Of course it was. Usually if she was visiting Lexi, she would press the button on the outside and speak to her and she'd buzz her in.

"Great, now what? Where's your vehicle?" Elliot asked.

"I left it back at my apartment in Bushwick."

"So why are we here?" Damon asked.

"Because my bag of belongings is here."

"And you have none at your home?"

Her eyebrows arched. "I need to find out if my friend is still alive," she said feeling as though she was having to justify herself. It's not like they needed to follow. In fact she didn't expect the other two to come along, and the only reason she invited Elliot was because he seemed pretty sure that whatever had occurred wasn't an isolated incident and being that her family was across the other side of the country, her friends were nowhere to be found and her lunatic ex-boyfriend was probably waiting for her to return to her apartment, she didn't feel comfortable walking back alone. Not that she was convinced that either of them weren't dangerous, but she got a sense from the way they helped others in Times Square that they were good people, even if they were hesitant to speak about their lives. It felt like she was trying to pry blood from a stone getting Elliot or Damon to open up, however, Jesse was the complete opposite, she couldn't get him to shut up. She wouldn't have minded if he had something useful to add but he hadn't stopped bellyaching since Times Square.

* * *

"Give me a boost up," Jesse said turning to Damon.

"Probably best I go, you're a short ass," he said reaching up as Jesse bent down and gave him a boost to grab the steel ladder. He dragged it down and then started to make the ascent.

"What apartment is she in?"

"Fifth floor, the one on the right."

"Okay, you wait down here."

"I'll go with you," Elliot said following him up. Damon led the way, his boots clanging against the steel. A couple of people peered out of their apartment windows obviously wondering what all the racket was. From four stories up, he could get a better look at the surrounding area. Several fires had been started throughout the city. It was hard to know if they were from a downed plane or looters. He looked down towards Maggie. She reminded him of his daughter, and in some ways, if his daughter had been far from home and an event like this had played out, he would have been glad to know that someone had helped her. That's why he changed his mind, that and of course he was hoping she would let him use her car, or at least drive him the distance back to Lake Placid. Of course he realized that was a lot to ask but based on the way she was acting back at Times Square, he had a good sense that she wasn't the type of person that would turn her back on those in need, even though he'd convinced her there was nothing that could be done.

When they reached the fifth story, Damon tapped on the window a few times to see if anyone was inside. Elliot shone his light into the apartment. The curtains were open and they could see that no one was in the living room. Another knock and still nothing that's when Damon tried the window. It was locked. He shrugged. "Oh well, guess they're not there."

He brushed past Elliot and before he'd made it down one flight of steps, Elliot used his elbow to smash the window. A quick jab and shards of glass went everywhere.

"What the hell?"

"She wants in, we're in," he replied before lifting the window and climbing inside. Glass crunched beneath his boots.

"Hello?" Elliot called out just in case someone was inside. The last thing he wanted to do was spook them and find himself staring down a gun barrel. When there was no sound he moved in with Damon close behind. He unlocked the door and told him to go down and let the other two in. As Damon disappeared into the darkness and he heard him jogging down the steps, Elliot shone the light around the apartment. It wasn't much to look at. A two-bedroom place, open kitchen and small living area, just enough room for a couple or three students. He walked over to a side table and picked up a photo frame. It contained a photo of a girl no older than twenty-two in a bikini on a beach alongside a beefy-looking guy. He placed it down and headed into the kitchen where he looked in the fridge. The light never came on, and all the food inside would soon spoil. He reached in and grabbed out a pack of ham. He tore it open and pulled out a few slices to chew on while he checked out the rest of the place.

Jesse was the first one in the door followed by Maggie.

"Really, Elliot? She is going to kill me!"

"Your friend probably didn't make it," he replied before scooping another slice of ham into his mouth.

"Don't say that. And put that away. That's not yours to take."

He chuckled and tossed it on the counter. Maggie

hobbled in and placed it back in the fridge. After doing so she winced in pain and gripped her leg.

"Here, let me give you a hand," Elliot said.

"I'm fine."

"We'll need to stitch it up. I can do it."

"I would rather bear the pain, thanks."

"Suit yourself but you do need to change the bandage otherwise it will become infected. Now you want to grab your bag and we'll head out."

"I'm not going back to my apartment. Not with my ex on the loose."

All three of them looked at one another. "I think you'll be fine. Let's go."

"No, I'm going to wait here until they get back."

"What about the ride?" Elliot asked.

"Um, maybe I shouldn't have offered that."

"So you've changed your mind?"

"Look, I appreciate you guys bringing me back but I don't know you, hell, none of us know each other," she said before taking a seat at the kitchen table. Elliot swallowed the remainder of the ham in his mouth and went over to the sink and turned on the faucet. It spat out some water, and he turned it off.

"And what happens if they don't come back?" Elliot asked pulling out his cigarettes and lighting one up. Damon eyed them, and he tossed him one.

"Then, I..."

She had no idea. The truth was no one really did as without a means of communicating, there was no way to tell if this was isolated to New York or had affected the rest of America.

"It's not safe to stay here."

"I'll be fine," she replied.

Elliot stuck the cigarette in the corner of his mouth, reached into his bag and tossed her a bandage. "Jesse, remove the old one and use this one."

"I can do it myself," Maggie said acting all uppity. He shrugged and lugged his backpack over his shoulder and headed towards the door.

"Where are you going?"

Without looking back he said, "The roof. I want to get a better idea of what's going on out there."

"I think we already know," Jesse said. "I haven't seen one light on in the whole journey here." Elliot didn't listen to him as he headed out the front door and climbed the stairs taking two at a time. Behind him he heard footsteps, and he turned to find Damon following him. He didn't bother to say anything. When they made it to the top floor, he pushed against the fire escape exit and walked out onto the roof. There were a few aluminum vents, and some cord strung between them as if someone had used it for laundry. It was still dark out and was closing in on one in the morning. He dropped his bag and unzipped it and Damon watched him intently. Elliot reached in and pulled out a small pair of binoculars. He lifted them to his eyes and took in the sight of Brooklyn. For as far as the eye could see it was total darkness. The only light came from the moon and stars.

"You really think it was a nuke?" Damon asked.

"No but I'm pretty sure it's an EMP."

"How sure?"

"A hundred percent. Vehicles and cell phones don't just stop working when a guy hits the wrong switch," he replied bringing the binoculars down. He took a hard pull on his cigarette and then crouched down to put the binoculars back in the bag. As he moved stuff around, Damon caught sight of the Glock 17.

"You brought a gun?"

He glanced up at him. "You sound surprised?"

"I just… why do you need that?"

"I might not need it but it's there if and when I do."

"How long have you been in New York?"

"A year, two months, and fourteen days."

"Sounds like a sentence," Damon replied.

"And when were you released?" Elliot asked. Damon shot him a glance as if confused. Elliot clarified. "I've met a number of people from Rikers. They all carried the same brown paper bag."

Damon glanced down at his pocket where it was sticking out.

"I was going to tell you."

"Doesn't matter. None of my business," Elliot replied glancing at him before reaching into his bag and producing a map and compass. He laid them out on the ground, placed a small flashlight between his teeth and checked a few things before folding the map back up again and squeezing it back inside.

"I did eight months inside. Cocaine possession."

"You clean now?"

"I was never on it," Damon said taking a seat on the edge of the building and puffing away on the cigarette. "A good friend of mine told me I was picking up parts for the garage. We run a business together back in Keene."

"And let me guess, he forgot to tell you about what was stashed inside?"

"You seen that before?"

"In Iraq."

"What are you, a Marine?"

"Army. I did sixteen years before I was given a medical discharge."

"Huh!" Damon said wiping his lips with the back of his sleeve. "You know, I always thought about enlisting. Yeah, my old man was in the Marines. He was always harping on about serving the country and whatnot."

"And?"

Damon spat over the side of the building before taking another drag. "I just never got around to it. Had me a girl back in Keene. She didn't want me to go and Cole, my buddy, the same one that got me into this, well he had all these ideas for us to open up a shop together. I just didn't realize he was going to run a side business."

"Shit happens," Elliot said. His mouth formed a smile and Damon nodded. "So you didn't throw him under the bus?"

"I thought about it," he said. "There were definitely days when I was inside that I contemplated speaking to a lawyer and making a plea deal where I could get a reduced sentence, but I couldn't do it. We go way back. I know if he was in my shoes he would have done the same."

Elliot stared into his eyes. "You sure about that?"

Damon must have become uncomfortable as he turned the topic back to his bag. "So what else you got in there?"

"Basics. Walking shoes, hat to keep warm, a rain jacket, gloves, knife, multi-tool set, headlamp with spare batteries, dust mask, water and purifying tablets, blood-stopping bandage, a tarp for shelter, my Glock, first-aid kit, spare ammo, meal replacement bars, energy booster, lighter, pen and paper, paracord and duct tape."

"You one of those prepper types?"

"Nope, just an ordinary guy taking precautions."

Damon nodded. "You think her vehicle will start?"

"Won't know until I see it."

"So you got family back in Lake Placid?"

"A wife and two kids."

"You divorced?" Damon asked.

"Nope."

Silence stretched between them as Elliot loomed over his bag, taking inventory just to be sure no one had found it and stolen anything. He squinted as smoke from his cigarette spiraled up into his eye.

"So what brought you this way?"

The question brought thoughts to his mind of returning from his last deployment overseas. It had been more difficult than the previous three before that. He'd lost many of his close friends and had witnessed atrocities done against Americans and Iraqis that he couldn't erase from his mind, but it wasn't just that.

His mind snapped back to being trapped inside an armored personnel carrier after it took a direct hit from an RPG. The explosion was deafening, and then when it caught fire that's when things went really bad. Elliot recalled being one of the last to crawl out but then realizing one of his buddies was still trapped underneath twisted metal. As they came under heavy fire, he'd slipped back in to try and get him out, but it was impossible. He still bore the burns on his arms from trying to pull him away from the hot aluminum. The agony as the flames consumed his friend was so bad that he'd asked Elliot to kill him. In a final act of mercy to end his suffering, Elliot shot him in the head. At least that's how he saw it, he wasn't sure if anyone else would ever understand

After that, he was never the same. It had broken something inside of him. Depression, guilt, traumatic night terrors and rage took over as he tried to deal with the grief of his death, and he quickly spiraled down into self-hatred and loathing.

He always thought he was stronger. He'd heard stories of vets suffering from PTSD but he always thought it was just in their head. Nothing more than a crutch they leaned upon after they returned to a world that no longer saw them for who they were — a soldier. He soon realized that wasn't the case after the nightmares started. Coming to terms with being a father at home and looking for work only added to the stress.

After seeking help at the urging of Rayna and Gary, he'd started attending group therapy sessions and had even got Kong. That dog had meant a lot to him. He could sense when Elliot was losing his cool, and he had this way of calming him. Just the thought of Kong made his heart ache. He'd contemplated bringing him along to

New York, but he didn't think it was fair. Back then he could barely look after himself let alone a dog.

Still, for a time the therapy worked. He met other vets facing PTSD, and he began to feel he wasn't alone. There were good days and bad and when it was bad, it was really bad. The nightmares were hard to endure, the vivid memories and flashbacks felt like he was reliving it all over again. Although he had the meetings, it didn't take long before he stopped going and started to withdraw and feel emotionally cut off from his own kids and wife. Now had that been all that had happened, he might have still been in Lake Placid, but it wasn't.

Crack!

The sound of gunfire.

Both of them whipped their heads around.

Two shots were followed by a scream. He didn't even have to say anything to Damon, they both took off, heading back to the apartment.

# Chapter 11

Elliot pulled the Glock from his bag and double-timed it across the roof with Damon right behind him. They entered the stairwell and quickly made their way down until he had the apartment door in sight. There was a large hole in the door as if someone had kicked it in. He threw up a hand to let Damon know to stop. He didn't want to go charging in there without knowing what he was up against. Was it looters? An armed group? Hugging the wall with his back he inched his way down, hearing two male voices, one of which was Jesse's.

"Calm down," Jesse said.

"Is this who you've been screwing? Huh?" an unidentified male's voice barked. After what she said about her boyfriend, Elliot figured he'd made his way over.

"Eric, just get out."

"Where is that bitch?"

"Lexi's not here."

"You're coming with me."

"She's not going anywhere," Jesse said.

"Did I tell you to speak?"

Elliot continued getting closer, his finger resting outside of the trigger. Calmly he made his way closer to the door that was partially closed, he slowed his breathing to control his nerves. It wasn't like he hadn't entered a building and faced off against someone who was armed. He'd done it many times in Iraq but that was then, this was now. He certainly didn't want to kill another person, not after all he'd been through but if that's what it came down to, then so be it.

"Just let him go, Eric. He has nothing to do with this."

"Oh he has everything to do with this. Who else have you been screwing?"

Elliot caught sight of Jesse through the crack of the door. He got up from the couch and a large guy with a shaven head shoved him back down. "Look, man, just leave her alone."

"Nathan, keep on him, me and Maggie are going to have words out back."

"Hey!" Jesse said before he was whipped across the face with a gun. *Shit.* Two of them and at least one of them was armed. He figured the other was as well. He could still hear Maggie talking, her voice slightly muffled but clear enough to make out the conversation.

"You can forget going home. Everything you have is outside. And I mean everything. All I wanted to do was talk but you had to be the bitch."

Elliot heard a slap, then crying.

"Do that again and I promise, I will…"

"You'll what? Hit me? Go on. Do it. It will be the last time you do."

Damon slipped past Elliot and took a position close to the wall on one side of the door while Elliot took the other. He knew this could go wrong and he didn't want to risk Maggie getting hurt. Gary had told Elliot about the types of domestics he'd been called out to and how quickly things could go south. Then again, he knew he if didn't get in there fast both of them could be harmed.

"Oh Maggie, I'm not going to harm you but your little boyfriend out there. He's open game."

"He's not my boyfriend."

"Then who is he?"

"Someone I met in Times Square when I was out with Lexi."

"Yeah? Where is she then?"

"How the hell should I know? I was thrown into a police van. The last I saw she was making a dash for it. Before…"

"Before what?"

"Before the lights went out and a plane came down."

The guy started laughing. "Oh that's fresh even for you. Plane came down? Please."

"It's true."

There was a thud.

She cried again as if he'd shoved her up against a wall. "Stop lying. You always fucking lie! Why did you have to change?"

"Change? You're the one who lifted a hand to me."

"Because you wouldn't listen. How the hell do you expect me to get through to you when you are always yapping? Nagging? Now you're going watch while I deal with your boyfriend. This is on you."

"Eric, no."

Elliot heard a commotion in the back and then another slap. That was enough. He kicked the door wide and took aim, but instead of firing off a round he shouted at the guy.

"Put it down!"

The guy was startled but not stupid enough to think he could fire off a round before Elliot pulled the trigger. "Okay, okay, man. Calm down."

He watched as the guy crouched and lowered the piece to the ground.

"Elliot!"

Two rounds were fired through the door from behind it by Eric. Elliot pulled back and readjusted his position so that the wall was blocking him. That's when he saw the guy go for the gun on the ground. "Don't...!" Before he could spit the rest of the words out, Elliot unloaded a round into him, followed by a second. The first round caught him in the chest, and the second hit him in the abdomen. His body twisted and dropped. From inside the apartment he heard the other guy cry out.

"Nathan!"

Eric ran into view, dropping his handgun on the ground beside him so he could scoop up the guy on the floor. He rocked him in his arms. "No. No. No. Nathan. Nathan!"

He didn't die immediately, blood trickled out the corner of his mouth and he coughed a few times trying to say something to Eric. Then, quickly his eyes glazed over and he was gone.

*Shit,* he thought.

Elliot moved in fast and kicked away Eric's gun while keeping his own weapon trained on him. Jesse was quick to retrieve Nathan's weapon while Damon went and got the other one.

"Nathan," he said, his voice becoming softer with the realization that he was dead. He ran his hand over his hair, a bloody mess, causing it to become matted. Eric turned his face towards Elliot, tears streaking his cheeks. "You just killed my brother."

"I warned him."

Eric gritted his teeth and lowered Nathan's body on the floor and then staggered to his feet. "Stay down," Elliot said but Eric ignored him. He got up and stared at the blood soaking his hands. Shock was setting in as his skin turned a pasty white. His face twisted, rage filling his expression before he burst forward and Elliot smacked him across the jaw as hard as he could with the butt of the handgun. Eric hit the ground, out cold. Elliot wasn't going to kill another person, especially not one that wasn't armed.

Elliot's gaze swiveled to Maggie who had now come out of the other room and repeated what he'd told Eric. "I warned him."

"I know you did." She looked down at Nathan then

Eric with a look of despair, it soon turned to fear. "We need to get out of here." She brought a hand up to her head, then scooped up her bag of belongings and headed towards the door. They all backed out and made their way down the stairs, even as several people came out of their apartments after hearing the commotion and gunfire.

"Maggie, you okay?" Jesse asked trying to keep up with her. For someone whose leg had a gash in it, she was moving faster than them.

"The police are going to come and…"

"The police won't show up," Elliot said as he caught up with her. "They're too damn busy."

She was moving at a fair pace and then she stopped, turned and slammed her fist against Elliot's chest. "Why? Why did you have to do that?"

"I told you."

"I know but… why?"

"He would have shot him, Maggie," Damon said, coming to Elliot's defense. "And Jesse, maybe you as well." She rubbed a hand over her face and looked on the verge of crying again. She stood there in the middle of the street for a second trying to calm herself before continuing on. Few words were exchanged on the way over to her apartment. Jesse wanted to head to his place but after what had just happened he was quick to change his tune. He tucked the piece he'd taken from Nathan into the front of his pants and covered it with his top. "Now all of us are going down for this."

"I just told you. The police won't do anything."

"How can you be sure?"

"God, I don't know how many times I have to say this. No matter how you look at it, and no matter who or what has caused the blackout. We're not going to bounce back from this within the next week, month or even a year without any power. So, you can kiss goodbye to emergency services as whatever infrastructure is in place will eventually fall apart once they realize the full extent of the disaster." He sighed. "Look, let's just get to her place, find out if this vehicle works and..."

"And what? Leave? Go where?" Jesse said. "Thanks to this, Maggie can't stay here now. Hell, even I can't."

"I just told you, the police…"

"Yeah, yeah, I heard."

Elliot stopped walking and thumbed over his shoulder. "What, you want me to go back and kill him? Is that what you're saying?" Elliot barked.

"No. I'm just…"

"I just saved your ass back there. Where I come from, most people say thank you."

Jesse exhaled hard and pressed on following the road around. The roads were filled with people who had come out to see what was being done about the blackout. Elliot knew this was just the beginning. People wouldn't immediately start hurting one another. No, they were used to the government fixing things. Their taxes paid for it, so there was this sense of entitlement, an expectation that all would be well even if it wouldn't. It was that delay he was relying on to get home safely because once the penny finally dropped, people would start to panic as food began to spoil, as supermarkets no longer stocked food and everything that people had come to rely upon no longer functioned. Then things would get really bad. Those who would have never thought about turning on their neighbor would change, and not for the better. He believed the American people were strong and most would try to help one another but it would have been foolish to think it would stay that way. In the end it would come down to survival of the strongest. Elliot could see Maggie wrestling with what had just taken place. She, like many others, would have to come to terms with making split-second decisions and facing consequences.

"What about your parents?" Jesse asked Maggie.

"They live too far away."

"Brothers? Sisters?"

"I don't have any," she replied.

Although Elliot had no qualms about dropping Nathan because he'd threatened his own life, he couldn't help feel sorry for Maggie. And that in some ways he was responsible for the position she was now in.

"If your vehicle works, you could stay with us for a while, if you want?" He just blurted it out not thinking about the logistics of it or even what Rayna's response would be to him returning.

Her brow knit together. "Go to Lake Placid with you?"

"Well you did offer to drive."

"I said…" She groaned and he realized that she hadn't meant what she'd offered back in Times Square. It was said in the heat of the moment, probably expecting him to turn it down. People did it all the time in life.

"Well it's either that or you attempt to drive to Kansas to where your folks are and who knows what the state of the country is like out there," he added. "Up to you. But if you've changed your mind, tell me now."

"It's just that he might come back. Eric, I mean. I can't stay."

"I don't think he'll return, Maggie, but like I said, the offer is there. As for us, we just need a ride."

Maggie stopped walking and supported herself against

a beam. Jesse came up alongside her and placed his arm around her. “You okay?”

“Yeah, just feeling a little dizzy.”

“Loss of blood and tiredness,” Elliot said. He came around the other side and she put an arm over his shoulder and both he and Jesse lifted her and carried her for a short while. They had a two and a half mile journey ahead of them to get to her apartment in Bushwick, and although Elliot wasn’t sure if any of what they had gone through today was going to lead to something better, he had to try, if only for the sake of his family.

## Chapter 12

Maggie's station wagon was a complete write-off. What a state that vehicle was in when they arrived at her apartment. She figured Eric had gone to town on it with a sledgehammer as all the windows were shattered, the side mirrors were dangling from nothing more than a few wires, the seats had been torn to shreds; the tires had been slashed but worst of all, parts of the engine were scattered over the ground.

Jesse took a few steps back to read what he had scrawled along the side. He must have done it with lipstick as in thick pink letters was the word: WHORE.

"Well, I guess that rules out the ride," Damon said.

"Oh, I don't know, a lick of paint, tighten a few screws and a couple of tires and I think we'll be back in business again," Jesse said in a joking manner.

Damon tapped the top of the roof and ran his hand over what looked like blood. "This guy has some serious issues. How did you end up with him?"

Maggie didn't respond, she simply hurried up the stairs into her apartment while the rest of them followed. Her apartment, or what was left of it, was something to behold. Jesse had to give it to the guy, he knew how to send a message. Every window in the apartment was smashed, her mattress was out on the sidewalk, and he must have taken a saw to her table as it was literally cut in half. There were huge holes in the walls, door and even the floor. Jesse looked down and could see an old woman in the apartment below. He offered a thin smile, and she stuck up her middle finger at him.

He cast a glance outside the apartment and her bald-headed neighbor looked out then closed his door quickly. That was to be expected. With everything that had occurred with the blackout, and then this, he probably thought they were going to cause him trouble.

"Holy shit," Damon said picking up a vinyl record that had been snapped in half. "David Bowie? Really? Is nothing sacred?" Although Eric had gone berserk, Maggie seemed to be holding it together, at least outwardly. She yawned and slumped to the floor.

"You need some sleep," Jesse said. "We all do." He headed for the door. "My place is not far from here, you're welcome to come. All of you."

Elliot nodded and picked up a bottle of wine that hadn't been smashed. He tossed it around in his hand and smiled. "Well, I guess not everything is a loss."

His words fell on deaf ears. Maggie looked more than distraught, she looked numb. Jesse knew something about that. That's how he felt after Chloe died. It was like someone had taken a sledgehammer to his life. Without her it felt empty and meaningless.

They remained at her apartment for another ten minutes until Maggie could summon the strength to leave. She collected what little things hadn't been torn apart and stuffed them in her bag. It wasn't much. A couple pairs of pants, underwear, two tops and that was about it.

* * *

Jesse lived about six blocks from Maggie's place on Gates Avenue. It wasn't a bad apartment block, however it did attract a few drug users. He'd moved in there a month after losing Chloe because he couldn't bear to come home to their old apartment. He could smell her perfume, and everything reminded him of her. He stuck his key in the lock and twisted it and opened the door, beckoning the other three to enter. They strolled in and looked around, taking in the sight of his minimalistic abode. There wasn't much to it. A medium-size living area, a sofa bed that he also used as his couch, a tiny kitchen and an even smaller bathroom. He'd spent a bit of money updating the flooring and had eventually got around to adding curtains four months after moving in, but beyond that it was pretty basic, a lot like his life.

"It's not much but you can toss a few cushions on the floor and push those two chairs together."

"It's like a five-star hotel," Elliot said. "I mean, compared to where I was staying."

Jesse chuckled and then looked at Damon. He

shrugged. "It's bigger than my last place."

"Really?"

Damon looked at Elliot and he smiled. Jesse had a sense that Elliot was privy to something Damon hadn't told him or Maggie. Jesse tossed his keys on the counter and went over to the fridge. He reached in and pulled out a few bottles of Budweiser and handed them out. A quick twist of the top and he chugged his back in one go.

Although he wouldn't say it out loud, in many ways he was kind of glad that society had broken down. At least now they could feel a smidgen of what he'd felt over the past year since losing her.

Damon noticed the photograph of Chloe and him on a side table. "This your girl?"

He went to speak but Damon continued, "Now that's one to hold on to. Where is she?"

He dropped his head a little. "In Brooklyn cemetery."

The moment turned awkward. It was part of the reason he didn't tell anyone. There was nothing that killed the mood more than telling a stranger that his wife was dead.

"I'm sorry," Damon said placing the photo frame back down.

"It's okay, it was a while ago."

"How long?"

"January."

"That's not exactly a while ago," Elliot said sinking down into a chair. Jesse turned and closed the door behind him. It was a little after two in the morning. The sun would be up soon and well… he wasn't really sure what he was going to do. His life before the blackout wasn't exactly going to plan. If he was honest, he was coasting through life, just pushing through each day. Work was nothing more than a means to pay bills and keep his mind occupied. Pleasure? What pleasure? From sunup to sundown he spent his days working.

He headed over to the fridge and pulled out a few items: cheese, ham, veggie samosas and some of yesterday's pizza then left it on the counter for them to help themselves. Damon and Elliot took a few items and then settled on the floor for the night. He provided them with a blanket each. It wasn't much, but they didn't seem too fazed by it. In all honesty, they were all just too damn tired to care. He studied Elliot who rolled over and closed his eyes. He'd killed someone and yet it didn't seem to bother him. Had it been him, he would have been a wreck. Or would he? He took another sip of his drink and told Maggie she could have the couch. He laid a sleeping bag down nearby and crawled inside. Without any power, the apartment was cold, really cold. Temperatures had dropped to eleven degrees but felt like 10 degrees below zero in the wind.

"Do you mind me asking how it happened?" Maggie said catching him off-guard.

He was hesitant to reply but after all he'd witnessed about her life so far, he didn't think she'd be shocked by anything he told her. Then again, what would she think? That had been another reason why he didn't want to tell people because it would turn into a pity party and he didn't want people to pity him.

"On the way back from her mother's. The truck came out of nowhere and T-boned our vehicle. She was driving. She died, I lived. Not much more to say than that."

"And you were married?"

"Yeah, newly married."

"I'm sorry."

"That's what everyone says. Ah, it is what it is. So what's the deal with your ex? Eric. Surely he wasn't always like that."

She rolled onto her back and stared up at the ceiling. "No, he wasn't. It's not like I did anything different. We were seeing each other for two years and slowly over time he started to become controlling. You know. He wanted to know where I was going all the time. He didn't like me visiting my parents, or going out with friends. It was progressive, you could say. Almost unnoticeable. I just thought he wanted to spend more time together. Anyway, one thing led to another and he must have seen me out with friends as he accused me of cheating on him." She looked over at Jesse. "I didn't cheat on him. That's not my thing. It takes too much work."

"That's what I used to say to Chloe."

Maggie smiled then it faded.

She sighed. "One night I got home, and he just went ballistic. He lashed out and knocked me into the wall then stormed out. The next day he was all apologetic and shit, but I told him he had to leave."

"Good on you. Takes a lot of courage to do that. My sister had a friend who was in a similar position. She just kept letting the guy back into her life and he just did it again and again. Eventually she wound up in hospital on a life support machine."

Maggie nodded. "Yeah, my father always told me that getting angry is one thing. People have arguments in their relationships, but it crosses the line when they physically abuse. He didn't have any patience or sympathy for that. One strike and you are out, he told me. If a man ever hits you, you get out of that relationship as there will always be someone out there that will treat you better." She smiled.

"You still in touch with family?"

"Yeah. You?" she asked.

"No. My family broke up when I was young, and I didn't exactly have the best relationship with my father. My mother lives in Sacramento with some new guy."

"So what brought you out to New York?"

He glanced at the photo of Chloe and she nodded. "Right." Silence stretched between them. "So you were a bike messenger?"

"For the past year, before that I worked in banking. It was a well-paid job. High stress though. After losing Chloe I couldn't do it anymore. Might sound strange but when I was out there weaving between vehicles, I had no other choice than to focus on the road and pedestrians and cabs. It kept my mind occupied, you know?"

A few minutes passed, and she stifled a laugh.

"What's funny?"

"This. Lexi would be climbing the walls right now if she knew that I was with three strange men. She carried pepper spray wherever she went." She breathed in deeply, then snorted. "You know she even ended up spraying some hobo in the face thinking he was trying to grope her when all he wanted was a buck for coffee." She started to laugh, and he joined in. "Oh we are bad. I shouldn't laugh but… uh…" She trailed off and for the first time since the whole event kicked off, and losing Chloe, Jesse felt a connection. It wasn't a romantic connection but just a human one, one that everyone needed to feel. City life didn't exactly lend itself to being able to form connections with others. Sure, there was always some event, group or club he could have joined but on the few nights he thought about venturing out and meeting people he couldn't bring himself to do it. It was easier to keep people at a distance.

"Tomorrow. What are you going to do?" she asked.

He breathed in deeply and looked up at the ceiling. He really hadn't given it much thought. He knew that Elliot and Damon would be heading north but he didn't know if what had occurred earlier was reason enough for him to leave. He hadn't killed anyone. If the cops showed up, he could just act like he didn't know them. Then again what if Elliot was right? What if this was all just a precursor to something far worse? Instead of answering he turned towards her.

"Not sure. Are you really gonna go with them?"

"Elliot was saying this could get worse." She paused. "I really don't know what to do. I was thinking of heading back over to Lexi's place in the morning. Who knows, she might be back by then."

"I don't think that's a good idea."

She offered back a worried expression.

The conversation died there. Neither of them were in a good position, none of them really knew the full extent of what had occurred, only that if the power didn't come on, life wouldn't just become hard, it would get dangerous.

Jesse wasn't ready for that. Neither was Maggie. He glanced over at Elliot. But perhaps he was.

## Chapter 13

A lot can change in twenty-four hours, especially city that's already plagued by poverty, drugs and looking for the opportunity to take advantage of Jesse was awake before the others. He had a terribl of sleep. He'd only managed to get a few hours when he closed his eyes he kept seeing the Nathan. It was one thing to see a dead bo movies, another to see one two feet away. A th morning light seeped through the drapes. smelled stuffy, a mixture of male sweat and ga his back turned to the others he studied taken from Nathan. At no point in time ha one, let alone held one.

"Careful, you don't want to shoot yo said stepping over him and heading fo Jesse gave a nod. At the sound of him others woke. Maggie rubbed her eyes.

"How did you sleep?" Jesse asked.

"Surprisingly well."

Elliot reached for his cigarettes and tapped one out. Without Damon even asking, he took one out and tossed it onto his blanket before getting up and heading over to the window. He cracked it open and perched his butt on the ledge. A cold breeze blew in.

"What's it like out there?" Damon asked walking back in while zipping up his pants.

"Quiet," Elliot replied, lighting up his cigarette and ›lowing a plume of smoke out. "It won't stay like that, so ‹'s best we get going as soon as possible."

Jesse crawled out of his sleeping bag and headed into ıe kitchen to see what he could whip up for breakfast. ‹en though it was light out, he lit a candle inside the ırtment to provide more light. He was shivering, so he ıt into his closet and pulled out a thick sweater and ped it on.

Anyone else cold?"

Iaggie stuck a finger in the air and he tossed her a

sweater. Even though he hung on to Chloe's clothes for a few months after she passed, he eventually gave them away to a local secondhand store as he couldn't bear to keep looking at them. It was odd the range of emotions he went through after her death. There was a period when he didn't want anyone touching her stuff, not even her own family, then he allowed them to come in and take what they wanted just so they would have something to remind them of her. He glanced at his watch. It was a little after eight in the morning. He was pulling out some cereal when there was a knock at the door. Maggie eyed him and Elliot pulled his gun. Jesse crossed the room and peered through the peephole. He turned and told Elliot to put the gun away, it was his neighbor Bobby Riggs.

Jesse cracked the door open.

"Oh hey, Jesse. Heard you come in late last night. Everything okay?"

Bobby Riggs was an odd fellow. It didn't matter how clear Jesse made it that he didn't want to get into a long conversation with the man, he had this way of just showing up out of the blue and expecting him to drop whatever he had going on in his life.

"Fine, Bobby."

He peered over Jesse's shoulder. "Who's that?"

"A friend."

"Did you hear that explosion last night? I think it's what caused this blackout. I hope they get the electricity on soon as its freezing in my apartment. I checked with some of the other neighbors and it seems everyone is affected. You got power?"

"Nope," he replied, keeping his answers short and sweet otherwise it would lead into another question.

"So where d'you go last night? I thought we were going to see the New Year in together."

Jesse heard Damon chuckle a little behind him.

"I was in Times Square."

"Oh with your friend?"

"Friends." Damon and Elliot stepped forward and Bobby took a few steps back.

"Okay, well do you know what's going on?"

He didn't even want to mention an EMP as it would have led into a long-winded conversation and all he wanted to do right now was make some coffee, even if he was going to have to heat a pot by starting a small fire in his apartment.

"No idea."

"Well do you guys want some coffee?"

"Is it hot?" Elliot asked. Jesse squeezed the bridge of his nose. That was the worst thing he could say.

"Sure is. Used a Coleman camping stove. C'mon over."

Elliot slipped under Jesse's arm and grinned at him. He turned and asked the others if they wanted to go. There was no hesitation. They didn't know Bobby like he did. The last time he agreed to step in his apartment, he ended up spending six hours in there listening to him rattle on about politics and the state of the world. Jesse followed them into his place across the hall. Inside the smell of fresh coffee and weed dominated the air. That was one thing Bobby was into… weed and lots of it. He had his medical marijuana card and so a joint was never far from his hand. He had no problem with him smoking it but it smelled like shit. Real dank and pungent.

"Forgive the state. I had a few of the neighbors over last night. You know Barb and Marcus, Jesse?"

He nodded. He had no idea who the hell he was on about as other than Bobby he didn't converse with anyone else. He figured they were a new couple that had moved in that weren't familiar with Bobby's mental state. Maybe he was being a little hard on him, he was a nice guy, just a little odd. Inside his apartment it was the complete opposite of Jesse's. He was a bit of a hoarder and there was no theme to the place, unless clutter was a theme. He had two black leather sofas, matching armchairs, a huge statue of Buddha near his kitchen, Christmas decorations covering every inch of space and there was an oversized, black-and-white photo of Greta Garbo positioned above the couch.

"What happened to your leg?" Bobby asked Maggie as he went about pouring out four cups of coffee. Maggie looked down and then back at him. "A bit of an accident."

"I have some hydrogen peroxide and cotton balls in the bathroom you can use if you want to change that bandage."

Maggie tossed Elliot a look, and he nodded. Over the course of the next five minutes, Elliot went about cleaning her wound and bandaging it with a fresh one.

"Say, Bobby, you have a vehicle by any chance?" Damon asked.

"A moped."

"Right, that's not going to be of much use."

He brought a tray of coffees out into the living room and set it down on the table and then went about asking if anyone wanted cream and sugar. Coffee that morning tasted sweet. It was like having someone breathe life back into them.

"I noticed all the vehicles stalled on the road. What do you think could have done that?"

Elliot fed him a few answers, unaware that it would

only lead to more questions. While they chatted, Jesse went to the window and looked outside. Several people were on the streets, some carrying goods inside shopping carts and looking nervously over their shoulder. It was hard to know how long it would take for society to break down but if Elliot was right, the cities would be the worst place to be, especially if people started turning on each other out of desperation. He listened in on the conversation Elliot was having with Bobby and started to think that getting away from the city might not be a bad thing. It was not like he had reason to be there anymore. He'd been barely hanging on by a thread as it was. Another month or two and he would have probably sold up and headed for Florida. He'd always thought that owning a place by the beach, waking up to a warm weather instead of snow outside, would be a good thing. Heck, maybe he'd get a neighbor who'd leave him alone.

"So you recommend stocking up?" Bobby asked.

"Before an event, not after. It's a little late now."

Elliot finished up his coffee and seemed in a rush to

leave. "Look, thanks for the coffee but we've got to hit the road."

"Where are you going?"

"North. Lake Placid."

For once Bobby was quiet which was very out of character for him. It seemed clear that what Elliot had told him about the EMP had unnerved him. As each of them thanked him for the coffee and exited, Maggie appeared to be the only one concerned for his well-being.

"We're just going to leave him?"

"What do you expect us to do?" Damon asked. And there it was, the truth in the midst of a disaster. They were in the same position as Bobby, no better off, it wasn't up to them to make other people's lives any easier. Elliot asked if Jesse had any water before he headed out. He went and grabbed a couple of bottles from the fridge.

"Well this is it. It's been nice knowing you," Elliot said.

"I guess," Jesse said scratching the stubble on his face.

Elliot smirked then turned his attention to Maggie.

"My offer is still open. We'll be outside."

She smiled and both Elliot and Damon headed downstairs.

She turned to Jesse. "Why don't you come with us?"

"Me? There's nothing in Lake Placid for me. Besides, why do you want to go? You don't even know him. For all we know, he might be out of his mind. Look at him, Maggie. He's been sleeping on the street, and the other guy, Damon… well, who knows what his story is but I don't get a good feeling about it."

She got this sheepish look on her face and her chin dropped. "If this is what Elliot said, don't you think it's better to stick with someone who's familiar with how to survive this?"

Jesse sighed and leaned against the doorway.

"We don't even know what this is, Maggie. Heck, you don't know me. I don't know you."

"And so what, we ignore one another? Is that the answer?"

"Seems to work with my neighbor, Bobby."

"That's your way, not mine," she said. "Look, I'm not going to convince you to come with us. If you want to stay, stay." Her mouth curled up at the corner, a strained smile. "Nice to have met you, Jesse."

"Likewise," he said extending a hand. She shook it before heading down the steps. Jesse walked back into his apartment and closed the door behind him. He stared at the blankets on the ground and listened to his clock ticking. He eyed the photo of Chloe on the side table and went over and picked it up. His mind churned over what she would have wanted him to do. It wouldn't be the first crazy thing he'd ever done. Quitting a well-paid job in banking and taking a job as a bike messenger was right up there, as was eloping with Chloe to Vegas. Jesse walked over to the window and looked out. Down below he saw Maggie exit the apartment block. She glanced up for a second and he gave a nod before she joined the other two. Elliot lifted his eyes, then they continued on their way heading west.

Jesse tapped the frame of the window with his

knuckles for a second or two and then turned back to his empty apartment. *Oh, what the hell,* he thought. He scooped up his sleeping bag, stuffed it in his backpack and grabbed the flashlight off the counter, and a few things to eat, before heading towards the door. He was about to leave then remembered the gun he'd left on the counter.

"Let's hope I don't need this," he said scooping it up and heading out.

Outside he knocked on Bobby's door. Bobby answered with a smile on his face, thinking that he'd come over to spend time with him. Instead, he tossed him his keys.

"Keep an eye on my place, okay? I might be back in a few days. I might not be back at all."

"What?"

"See yah later, Bobby!"

He hurried down the steps and double-timed it to catch up with them.

## Chapter 14

When morning came, Rayna awoke to a large, heavy weight pressing down on her legs. She groaned and tried to move but she couldn't. Prying her eyes open, she looked and could see that Kong had decided to plonk his butt down on her legs. He was stretched over fast asleep.

"Kong, get off."

An ear went up and one eye opened. The dog let out a big yawn, then slid off the end of her legs.

"That's right, take your time."

She looked over to her kids who were still sleeping before she gazed at the digital clock. Damn it! The power hadn't come on. She hadn't slept much that night. The encounter with her neighbors at midnight had put her nerves on edge and so she found herself waking up to even the faintest creak. She slipped out from her blankets and looked outside. At least the rain had stopped. She shook Lily.

"Come on, lazybones, get up. Lots to get done today."

"But it's a holiday."

"And I need your help around the house."

"Why's it so cold?" Evan asked.

"The heating isn't working."

She went out to the bathroom and turned on the faucet. It spluttered a few times and kicked out what remained inside the pipes. It wasn't much but fortunately she'd already filled the sinks and bath tub the day before. She went about washing herself and reminded the kids not to get rid of the water in the sink. She sat down on the toilet and relieved herself, then realized in that moment that no water meant… no flushing. Oh great. Of course there were plenty of streams, plus East Lake and Mirror Lake nearby that they could draw water from, but regardless, this wasn't good. Not at all. After she flushed the toilet for the last time, she headed downstairs and went through the process of checking the landline phone. Nothing. She yawned and stretched out, Kong did the same. Next she put on her boots and coat and headed outside towards the shed. She'd planned on getting the two-way radio before the men had shown up. She needed to get in contact with Gary and find out what was going on. Then it dawned on her. He probably wouldn't have the other headset on. Halfway across the yard she headed back into the house.

"Come on, kids. We're heading out."

Even though things were pointing to an EMP, her mind still wasn't jumping to that conclusion. Lily and Evan trudged down the stairs.

"But we haven't even had anything to eat."

"Grab a granola bar and banana."

"Where are we going?"

"To see Uncle Gary."

That's what they called him even though he wasn't related. Gary and Jill had been their closest friends for the longest time. In many ways, after seeing how Gary bounced back from PTSD, it gave her hope for Elliot, until he upped and left. Even then Gary still held out hope for him. "Give him time, Rayna. He'll come around," he said.

Except he hadn't. After twelve months without seeing him, she didn't know if he was alive or dead. Suicide rates were high among those suffering from PTSD and if she was completely honest with herself, the thought had gone through her mind that maybe, just maybe he'd reached that point.

Once the kids were dressed and ready to head out, she clipped a chain on Kong and locked up. Evan held on to Kong while she tried firing up her SUV. It hadn't started the day before but she just wanted to try it one more time. Nothing happened.

"What's going on, Mom?" Lily asked.

"It's okay, we're going to walk."

"Walk? But that will take us half an hour and it's cold."

"The exercise will do us good."

She locked up, and they headed off. As they came out of the driveway that's when she saw got a glimpse of what occurred yesterday. Farther down the road, vehicles were clogging up the street. These hadn't been parked. They were stalled. She saw a couple of her neighbors and waved to them. They offered back strained smiles but looked equally perplexed. It was only when she walked past the home of the two men, Austin and Trent, that she got nervous. Fortunately they weren't outside, but an old truck was, parked at an angle. She didn't like leaving the house unattended but until she spoke with Gary, she didn't know what she was up against.

Mirror Lake Drive circled around the perimeter of the lake then connected with Main Street on the west side. They headed south because the police department was just off Mirror Lake Drive and Parkside. Gary's place wasn't more than half a mile from there. They'd recently bought a beautiful home on Morningside Drive. It was nestled in the trees and backed onto Lake Placid Golf Club. She figured he'd be down at the station after the blackout.

## Chapter 15

It was a chaotic scene at the police station. The department was located in a three-story, brown brick building that also served as city hall, the mayor's office and the courts. That morning there had to be close to sixty people huddled outside in the cold wanting to voice their complaints and get answers about what was going on and why the power was off.

"Stay close," Rayna said gripping Lily's hand and elbowing her way to the front with Evan on her other side. She had managed to make it to the front doors when Officer Jackson prevented her from going in.

"Ma'am, I need you to stay outside."

"I'm here to see Gary Westin."

"He's a little busy at the moment."

"Can you please just pass on a message? Tell him it's Rayna Wilson. I need to speak to him."

He nodded and made a gesture for her to stand back.

She wasn't familiar with all the officers. Rayna had only met a few of them. The department wasn't large. There were eight patrolmen, one part-time patrolman, a sergeant, an assistant chief and the chief. She walked off to one side and huddled together with the kids. Kong sat down beside her and joined them observing the rabble of men and women voicing their complaints.

"How am I meant to feed my kids? None of the grocery stores are open."

"My mother is eighty-nine, she won't last through another night of these low temperatures."

A bulky man wearing a hunting cap and jacket shoved his way to the front and stabbed his finger into the chest of Officer Jackson. "I want to know right now what is going on. Why is the power out?"

"Sir, step back."

He took one step back but continued his tirade. "You know my taxes pay your salary. Now I know you aren't telling us something. So what the hell is going on?"

Officer Jackson was doing his best along with three

other officers to field questions and reassure the angry mob that every step was being taken to remedy the situation.

"This is North Korea, isn't it?" a woman shouted from the crowd. That only incited more yelling. She understood their frustration. It was very real. Fortunately, she had been to the grocery the night before the power went out, and Elliot had more than enough in the shelter to carry them for the next six months, but these people, well, she couldn't help feel their pain. Elliot had warned her about this kind of thing happening. He said society wouldn't collapse overnight but it wouldn't take long. Just because one person could reel in their emotions and act like a human being, it didn't mean others would do the same. And it would be foolish to think they would.

"Mom," Evan tugged on her jacket and motioned to three guys coming down the street with rifles on their backs. Each of them looked like they were hunters. She'd seen them around town driving a large truck. She glanced over to Officer Jackson but several of the officers had already spotted them. They drew their weapons and in a controlled manner pushed through the crowd and told the three men to put down their weapons.

"We have the right to bear arms."

"Concealed carry, not open. Now put them on the ground."

It was a tense few moments and after some back and forth the men lowered their weapons and the cops moved in, cuffed them and took them into the station. That again only made matters worse as others protested and said that they weren't doing any harm. Jackson looked at Rayna before following the other officers inside and closing the front doors.

She must have waited out there for close to thirty minutes before Gary emerged. Gary Westin was close in age to Elliot. Both of them were in their late forties. Gary was six foot two with cropped dark hair and a mustache.

"Rayna."

"Sorry to bother you, Gary, but I need to speak to you."

He cast a stern glance at the crowd and motioned for her to head inside with him.

"Looks like you have your work cut out for you," she said.

"Oh it's been manic since yesterday. People can't get through by phone so they've been showing up at all hours. There isn't anything we're able to tell them other than to go back home and wait for an announcement."

"Announcement?"

"The mayor will have a town hall meeting to address people's concerns. Officers will be patrolling along with volunteers near the grocery and pharmacy stores to prevent anyone from looting. They will set in place a six o'clock curfew. Pretty standard stuff."

He led her down a corridor and she glanced into the offices, which were packed with people discussing the situation.

"Everything okay at home?"

"Yeah, as good as it can be."

He motioned for her to head into his office.

"How you doing, kids?" They both mumbled under their breath and he ran his hand over Evan's hair. "And I see you brought Kong with you. Hey boy!" he said crouching down and running his fingers through the dog's hair. He rose and shut the blinds in his office for a little privacy.

"So what can I do for you?"

"This is an EMP, right?"

He stared back at her and then went around his table and took a seat.

"Um," he cleared his throat. "From what we can tell, yeah. No one has managed to find out what caused it so far, as TV, radio, everything is down and without a vehicle working we are kind of cut off from the outside world." He frowned. "Can I get you a coffee?"

"The vending machine is working?"

"No, but a camp stove is."

"It's okay, I'm fine." She leaned back in her chair and ran a hand over her face. "Last night when the lights went out. Two of my neighbors came by."

He shook his head and leaned forward. “And?”

“At midnight, in the rain.”

“What did they want?”

“They said they were checking. You know, seeing who else didn’t have power but…”

“But what?”

She shrugged and cast a glance at Lily. “I don’t know. I just get a bad vibe from them. One of them asked if it was just me and the kids.”

“And you said?”

“I didn’t reply. I told them to go on their way. I was holding a rifle.”

“Holding a rifle?” He smirked.

“Well, Elliot said.”

Gary sighed and rubbed the bridge of his nose. “You heard from him?”

“No. Nothing.”

He leaned back in his leather chair and ran a hand around the back of his neck. It was clear he was stressed.

“Listen, if you want to bring the kids to our house, I’m

sure Jill wouldn't mind."

"Actually, I was thinking that maybe you both wanted to head to the shelter."

He chuckled. "I think that would be kinda jumping the gun right now. Besides, I have a lot of work to do here."

"Like what?"

"Just because the power is out, Rayna, it doesn't mean the world comes to an end. There are folks out there who are still relying on us for protection."

"And how are you supposed to do that without any vehicles?"

He exhaled hard. "It's not going to be easy. Some of us will patrol on bicycle, the rest on foot. We're working with the community to find older vehicles that might operate. We still have a job to do. We have several volunteers in the community that will be assisting down here so we can be out there but yeah that's the plan so far."

"What about ham radio?"

"For?"

"To find out what's going on out there. We have one. Radio might be down but ham radio should be working. At least according to..."

"... Elliot," he finished what she was about to say. "Rayna, I know and we will get around to that. Right now we are just trying to deal with the backlash from everyone and assess the situation, create a contingency plan and issue a state of emergency."

"So are you running a generator in here?"

He nodded. "The town hall here has been set up as a command center while we deal with this."

"And what about water and food?"

He blew out his cheeks. "That's what the town hall meeting is going to be about. They'll hand out information with instructions on what to do to make refrigerated items last. Probably by suggesting folks leave milk, frozen meat and leftovers outside. With all the cold weather we've been having it should last. We're also working with the grocery stores to see if we can arrange to have bottled water made available."

"And what if people get ill?"

"Rayna. I don't have all the answers. We have someone who is working on all of that right now. All I can tell you is that our officers are telling everyone to attend the meeting, and then questions will be answered."

She nodded and he smiled at Evan.

"Why don't you drop by and see Jill? I'm sure she'd appreciate the visit and it would certainly make me feel better knowing that she's not alone."

"And how long are you going to be?"

"However long it takes. We have guys who worked through the night. So I need to be here for now."

"And my neighbors?"

He exhaled hard. "Look. I'll have one of the officers swing by, okay, but I'm sure they are just like everyone else. A little nervous. If you head home later just be sure to lock your doors. I'll keep you updated."

She offered back a strained smile and thanked him. As she got up, he came around and gave her a hug. She felt his thumb rub the back of her neck under her hair. They'd grown quite close over the months that Elliot had been away, probably a little too close. He hadn't cheated on Jill but that was only because she wouldn't let him. She might have missed the company of a man in her bed, but she wasn't that low. She had morals and knew where to draw the line. However that hadn't stopped him from seeing where the boundary line ended.

"Oh by the way. Do you still have the other two-way radio?"

"It's at the house."

She nodded. "Okay."

As Rayna and the kids headed out, she noticed the crowd had gotten larger, wilder, and she knew it would only be a matter of time before they took matters into their own hands. She'd drop by and see Jill and see if she could convince her to come back to the shelter. If she declined, so be it. Either way, she planned on making sure her kids were safe. At the end of the day that was her only priority.

## Chapter 16

All it takes is one person to unravel a nation, just as it takes only one domino for the rest to fall. That's what Elliot told them that morning, and that's what they witnessed as they walked past a Walgreens Pharmacy. Someone had taken a forklift, peeled up the security gate and smashed right through the front door leaving it wide open. They watched as young and old went in and out returning with armfuls of milk, soft drinks, chips, candy, medication and hygiene products. No one stopped them, and no one would. Police and the National Guard were overwhelmed, if they were anywhere to be seen. In the past hour they hadn't come across one soldier. Without communication it would take days before there was any real attempt at providing relief. People weren't dumb, they knew that. That was why so many days after Katrina there was still chaos. It was why there was a delayed response, and it's also why looting happened only twenty-four hours after Hurricane Irma hit and took out three-quarters of the power in Florida. Sure, emergency services were out there but the need was too overwhelming, and this was more than just a power outage. If the nation was under attack by North Korea, the troops would be called to action, leaving police, store owners and homeowners to deal with the problem at hand.

As they rounded another corner they saw three kids running from a Foot Locker carrying boxes of sneakers that they would sell later.

If the power remained down for longer than a few months, and if other areas in the world had been attacked by North Korea, who knew when help would come? Of course, ordering a citywide curfew would be one of the first steps that the mayors of New York and other cities would try to put in place but enforcing it, well, that was another thing entirely. As they continued past a stretch of stores, Elliot could already see some of the measures that store owners had put in place. Someone had sprayed a warning sign in red paint across the front of a set of metal shutters: YOU LOOT, I SHOOT!

But it wasn't just looting that would be the problem — widespread violence would come hand in hand as the desperate took whatever steps necessary to gain what they needed, even if it meant mugging someone.

"I would advise you to keep your gun on the ready, and your eyes peeled for trouble. It's a long walk out of this city and chances are things are going to turn ugly real fast."

Elliot took the lead, Damon watched his six while Jesse stayed by Maggie's side. He had to admit his change of mind had surprised him. He wasn't offering them anything more than what they might find if they stayed but he got a sense that they were looking to him to see their way through it. He didn't want to burst their bubble. Sure he knew a little about surviving. The army had taught him enough, and he'd put in place a shelter and enough to ride out six months, but that was for his family. It was the bare minimum. Certainly not enough for others.

"We aren't walking this whole thing, are we?" Damon asked, his eyes scanning the windows of buildings. Elliot didn't reply. Several loud bangs followed by gunfire made him think of Iraq and all the times they'd rolled into villages searching for insurgents. The moments they burst into homes seeking cover, or carrying their wounded. It was loud, hot and there was no telling what was around the next corner.

"If we come across an older vehicle, you think you'd know how to hotwire it?" Elliot asked, eying Damon.

"Oh, because I was inside, you automatically think I..."

"Inside?" Maggie asked. It was bound to come out. Better now than when they were a hundred miles outside of the city. Fortunately, Elliot didn't have to be the one to explain, but he knew he would probably get blamed for not saying anything. The thing was, it wasn't his place and ex-cons didn't bother him. He'd rubbed shoulders with them enough over the past year.

"I did eight months in Rikers for drug possession."

"So you're some kind of dealer?"

"No, just a mug who trusted his best friend and ended up becoming the fall guy."

"I had a friend of mine who ended up there. Said it was bad," Jesse said out of the blue. "He ended up in solitary confinement. Said it was exactly what he needed to get his shit together."

"Why was he there?"

"Tax fraud. He had to do a year inside."

Right then, two rounds were fired, one of them ricocheted off metal and instinctively Elliot hit the ground. "Get down!" He sucked in a breath and made sure the others were okay before he peered around the vehicle to see what was going on. No one was shooting at them. Someone had fired a few rounds through a Pizza Deli window. They were now kicking the shattered glass and entering. He motioned with two fingers for them to get moving. They were only seeing the tip of the iceberg. By nightfall there was no telling how bad it would be. He wanted to put as much distance between the city and them as possible. It wouldn't be easy without a ride. He'd already mapped out the journey and figured it would take them close to a hundred hours on foot. Now he'd hiked and run a lot of miles when he was a soldier but covering 286 miles? He was even more determined to find a vehicle. There had to be at least one they could find. Not everyone could afford the newest models.

They continued on, crossing over Newtown Creek and heading north on Van Dam Street. It would take them across the Robert Kennedy Bridge, through Randall Island Park and straight through the middle of the Bronx. He figured it would take a good four hours before they managed to get through there. It was a dangerous place day or night, though if he had to walk through it, it was better in daylight hours.

"Hold up," Maggie said leaning against the wall. She grimaced while reaching down and rubbing her leg. Elliot looked back and realized this was going to take much longer if they had to keep stopping and starting.

"Look, why don't you stay here in the cemetery and

me and Damon will go search for a vehicle? Remind me when I get back to put some stitches in that leg of yours."

Her eyes widened.

First Calvary Cemetery was huge. He figured no one would be hanging out there. Anyone looking to take advantage of others would be in stores, homes and down back alleys waiting for unsuspecting looters they wanted to mug.

"Yeah, not sure that's a good idea."

"Well it's either that or we walk through the Bronx at night. Take your pick."

Jesse nodded. "I'll stay with her. Go on."

He put his arm around Maggie and led her into the mammoth cemetery with huge granite tombstones. The sky was a deep blue and there were only a handful of clouds in the air. How dangerous could it be in a cemetery? he thought as he watched the other two head on without them. Would they even come back?

## Chapter 17

"You know the chances of us finding a vehicle that operates is slim to none. But you already knew that, didn't you?" Damon said, eyeing him as they trudged on through Long Island City, an industrial area that ran along the East River in Queens.

"They're going to slow us down and besides I don't have the means to support either of them." He cast a glance at Damon. "And you, well, you're heading my way."

"Then why did you invite her to come along?"

"Because she offered a ride and well..." He shook his head. "Look, it doesn't matter, does it?"

"That depends."

"What do you mean?"

"If you can live with that. It's not something I would do."

Elliot stopped walking while Damon continued. He

stared at him. More guilt, that's all he needed. All that mattered to him now was Rayna and the kids, no one else. Hell, if anyone else mattered he wouldn't have spent the last year underground trying to avoid human connection.

They walked in silence for a while, taking in the sight of one store after another that had been looted. It was to be expected. Without power, looters knew there were no cameras so the only thing they were up against was a store owner with a gun and even that wasn't going to deter them.

"Oh, don't look now, Queensboro Correctional Facility," Elliot said looking to throw a verbal jab back at Damon after his "It's not something I would do" remark.

"Hilarious," Damon replied before pointing to a college up ahead. "I figure if we need to find some shitty cars, it will be in there. College kids are notorious for scraping the bottom of the barrel."

"Even better, an indoor parking garage," he said as they came around onto Thomas Avenue. As they got closer, they noticed the sign in the window of the building beside it. It was the New York Army National Guard Career Center. Beside that was a sign that read: ALWAYS READY.

"Oh yeah, always ready. Where the hell are they?"

The streets were filled with people, but no police and no guardsmen. They crossed the street and jogged down the slope into the parking garage. Someone else must have had the same idea as the steel shutters had been pried up just enough for a car to squeeze out. Elliot pulled out his Glock and kept it low as they entered the garage. Damon swept his flashlight around as they went from car to car searching for one that looked like an old clunker. He realized it was like trying to find a needle in a haystack as even those who didn't have a lot of money drove vehicles from the '90s.

"What year are we looking for?"

"Ideally, the '70s but we might strike it lucky with one from the '80s."

They noticed that many of the vehicles had been

broken into. It was probably druggies looking for loose change, and tearing out audio equipment to sell.

"So you never told me why you ended up in New York."

Elliot shot him a glance. "I needed space."

"The old lady got on your nerves?"

"Not exactly."

"The kids piss you off?"

"No."

"Well it must have been pretty bad if you sought shelter in the tunnels of New York. That can't have been good."

"It's not that bad, actually."

"Why didn't you go to a shelter?"

Elliot scoffed. "You want to get robbed, have your throat slit or be sexually assaulted, by all means, check one out. Chat to anyone on the streets, they will tell you to avoid them at all costs. And the decent ones, well, you have to have been in the system for a while to qualify for those."

Damon squinted into the darkness, washing his flashlight over rear bumpers. "And I'm guessing you shied away from being in the system. Why?"

Elliot didn't like the constant barrage of questions. It was another reason why he avoided shelters, they asked too many questions, expected too much and were too damn nosy. At least below the streets of New York he could find solace, peace even. There were days he attended a group therapy session in the city, however he never went in. He would just stand outside and listen to the group talk. Most of them were vets, some survivors of traumatic sexual assaults. It was a mixed bag. Of course, there had been a few times the gal running it had spotted him and had welcomed him, but he couldn't go through that — sitting there in front of a bunch of strangers and pouring out his life to them. Nah, how was that going to help? It didn't take away the nightmares. It couldn't turn back the clock on what he'd done since returning.

His mind returned to that night, the flashbacks, Rayna's attempts to help him.

They'd had her brother and sister over for Thanksgiving. By any measure it should have been a good day. Kong had been by his side, keeping him from losing his cool even though internally he felt like he was losing grip on reality. Up to that point, he'd never had a visual flashback, just nightmares and depression.

*"Hon, I forgot to get the wine, can you do a run to the liquor store?"*

*"I'll take him," Keith said.*

*Keith was Rayna's younger brother. He was twenty nine with three kids.*

*It was a quick trip down the road. He wished he'd taken Kong with him. Maybe if he had, it would have ended differently. And maybe if he hadn't been carrying a concealed weapon, the outcome would have been different.*

Elliot's thoughts trailed, his mind snapping back and forth between the present and the event replaying.

*He recalled getting out of the Jeep and heading into the liquor store. Browsing through the bottles at the back of the store. The ring of a bell as someone else entered and then loud shouting, the commands to give money and a gun going off, then another round and glass shattering. After that it became a blur. All he could hear was mortars ringing in his head, his fellow soldiers yelling for help, he could see blood and…*

"Hey, Elliot, you okay?" Damon said snapping him out of his dreamlike state. "I think I found a vehicle. What do you think?"

He stepped back from a fair sized truck, the model was a Toyota Hilux, early '80s.

"If it worked, it wouldn't be here," Elliot replied before walking on.

"That or they left it here. We can at least try it, right?"

He shrugged still lost in the vague memories of the past. Usually when he felt this way he would drink, withdraw into the darkness of the tunnels and go a full twenty-four hours without seeing anyone. Before he could say anything, Damon used his elbow to smash the driver's side window. He then reached in and unlocked the door and slipped underneath to try and hotwire it. Elliot didn't get in but looked around, expecting a security guard to emerge at any minute, but no one came.

He heard the sound of sparks, a ticking sound, and then the roar of the engine.

"Hey, look at that!" Damon put his hand out and banged on the roof. "Get in."

Elliot slipped in the other side and wiped off shards of glass from the leather seat.

"You still want to leave them behind?" Damon asked.

Elliot thought about for a few seconds.

"No, let's go get them."

Damon chuckled. "There's hope for you yet, Elliot," he said with a grin on his face as he jammed the gear stick into drive and smashed the accelerator. They tore out of there with a new sense of hope, how long that would last was to be seen. There were only a few things valuable in a world without power — food, clean water, medication, shelter, weapons and transportation. They might as well have had a bull's-eye attached to their backs.

## Chapter 18

Maggie peeled back the bloodied bandage and took a look at the wound. It wasn't that bad, but it was going to need some stitches. Elliot had offered back at the house when he'd been cleaning it with the hydrogen peroxide, but she'd declined. She didn't deal with needles very well and that was just when she was visiting the doctor, but getting stitched up without an anesthetic, well that was too much to deal with. Her pain tolerance wasn't very high. *"It's all in your head. Just a mental game,"* Elliot had said. Yeah, right, she thought. It was easy for him to say as he wasn't the one who had to endure it. She shouldn't have told him that, though, as he ended up showing her two wounds from his time in Iraq.

"The shrapnel is still inside," he'd said pointing to his shoulder.

Jesse had walked a short distance away to take a leak. Every now and again she would look up and realize how strange it was to not hear vehicles driving by, or horns honking. The only sounds now were the odd gun going off, and the patter of feet as different people hurried down the street, probably escaping with stolen goods.

"So what did you do before this?" Jesse yelled, his head just visible above a gravestone. The steady sound of piss trickling followed.

"I did tech support for Dell."

"Dell? Didn't think that company was still in existence. I thought it had gone the way of the dinosaur like Microsoft."

"You do know that both are still around? Guessing you are a Mac user."

"Going on nine years," he replied as he emerged doing up his zipper. "So did you like it?" he asked.

"It was a means to an end."

"In this case, the end of the world, or the breakdown of New York," he said taking a seat beside her. "How's the leg?"

"Tender but I'll survive."

"You really should have let him stitch it up."

"Once he finds something stronger than bourbon, I might do that," she replied, squinting and then cupping a hand over her eyes to block the glare of the sun. Jesse brought his backpack around and unzipped it. He dug around inside for some fruit and offered her an apple.

"What else you got in there?"

"Oh just a few cans, some bottles of water, a lighter, a butter knife, stinky gym clothes and yesterday's newspaper."

"Sounds like a poor man's bug-out bag."

"Didn't exactly have time to pack," he said. He took a bite out of the apple and leaned back against the gravestone.

"What do you make of our ex-convict friend?"

Jesse squinted. "Seems harmless enough."

"But why wouldn't he tell us?"

"Would you?"

"Nah, I guess not."

"Everyone has their secrets."

"Yeah, I guess so," she replied. Out the corner of her eye she spotted a young girl making her way over to them. She couldn't have been more than twelve years of age with cornrows in her hair and wearing an Adidas tracksuit.

"Jesse," Maggie muttered. He sat up and looked, then reached for his gun.

"Put it away, she's just a kid."

He removed his hand and covered it up.

"Hello there," she said stopping about ten yards from them. "You wouldn't have any water, would you?"

Maggie went for the bag and Jesse put his hand on top of it. He was quick to speak up. "No, actually we don't, but if you walk six blocks, you'll find a pharmacy that has been looted. You might find a couple of bottles in there."

"And why would we want to do that?"

Jesse heard the click of a gun and smelled a smoker's breath near his face before he felt the gun press against the back of his head.

"Tonyah, take their bags, and oh," he said leaning

forward, "I'll take that."

He reached under Jesse's shirt and pulled out the Ruger revolver. Jesse squeezed his eyes shut, chiding himself for listening to Maggie. *Just a girl?* Stupid.

"Now what else you got?"

He still hadn't seen this man's face. The guy stayed behind him pressing the muzzle of the gun against his head.

Jesse kept his hands up. "That's it. You've cleaned us out."

"What's inside the bags, Tonyah?"

She unzipped them and started tossing out his belongings. "Just a bunch of shit."

"That's all?"

"Like I said, we weren't carrying much. Just take whatever you want."

"Both of you lie down on your stomach."

"C'mon, man, we don't have anything else."

"Am I not speaking English? Roll over!" he bellowed.

Jesse cast Maggie a look and then slipped forward.

"Hands behind your head and interlock your fingers."

They did as he said. Jesse turned his head and could now see the guy. He was a tweaker-looking dude. Wild eyes, dreadlocks and he kept licking his lips. He had several gold chains around his neck and tattoos across the front of his chest. He had the young girl check their pockets. All the while Jesse tried to make it clear that they weren't a threat, but it didn't seem to help.

"Shut the hell up!"

"Jerome, they ain't got anything, let's get the hell out of here."

"Well that's too bad." He came around to the front of them and kicked the bag across a few of the gravestones. "You won't be needing that anymore."

Maggie piped up. "Please, just..."

He fired off a round near her head. A chunk of soil kicked up and struck his face. "Seems ironic that these two assholes are going to die in a cemetery, don't it, Tonyah?"

Jesse heard the gun cock, and he squeezed his eyes shut

waiting for the end to come.

When the gun fired, he turned his head thinking that he'd shot Maggie first, but she was staring at the guy. Jesse turned his head towards their attacker and watched as he reached for his chest and then crumpled. The young girl bolted, dashing through the cemetery and disappearing into the tree line.

"Well, I go back on what I said about cemeteries not being a dangerous place," Damon said casually strolling up. Jesse turned to see both of them making their way up. Of course it had been Elliot who had shot the guy. Jesse breathed a sigh of relief. He had never been so pleased to see anyone in his whole life. He honestly thought he was going to die. They rose and brushed off the dirt. He stared down at the black guy's body and went over and took his gun back and relieved him of the one he was holding. Jesse offered it to Maggie, but she declined.

"I don't know how to use it."

"You'll need to learn," Elliot said. "Now how the hell did you get yourselves into this situation?"

Jesse looked at Maggie and her chin dropped. He cleared his throat and shifted his weight from one foot to the next.

"I didn't think the girl was a threat," he said speaking on her behalf. She glanced at him and the corner of her lip curled a little. "Anyway, how did you get on?"

"We've got a ride."

"The four wheels kind?" Maggie asked.

"Is there any other?"

"I was expecting you to show up with bicycles."

Damon rested his arm on a tombstone. "Ah, I hadn't thought about that."

Elliot stood nearby staring down at the body of the man he'd just shot. Maggie went over and touched his arm. "Elliot." She repeated his name again before he looked at her. He got this confused expression on his face that made it seem like he was somewhere else. What was his deal?

## Chapter 19

An hour later, Rayna sat inside Jill's kitchen drinking a hot cup of tea. She'd whipped it up using a camping stove from the garage, Rayna had helped dig it out. Now they both sat in a quiet kitchen watching Lily, Evan and Kong play in the next room. Gary and Jill didn't have kids, though it wasn't because they hadn't tried. Jill was unable to have kids.

"Thanks, Jill, this is nice," she said nursing the cup with both hands. Jill was in her late forties. A woman with high cheekbones, short curly hair with a sharp nose. That morning she was wearing blue jeans, flats and a white winter sweater. She wasn't a stickler for fashion and keeping up appearances like some folks she'd met, and perhaps that's why Rayna liked being around her. She didn't have to pretend.

"You know you and the kids are more than welcome to stay."

She smiled and nodded. “Actually, that’s why I’m here. Do you remember when Elliot built the shelter at the house?”

“Yeah, vaguely.”

“I was going through one of the notebooks that Elliot left behind. Everything that happened so far, corresponds with what he believed would have been an EMP.”

“A what?”

She smiled. “An electromagnetic pulse. Usually caused by a solar flare or a nuke.”

Jill put her cup down and reached across placing her hands on top of Rayna’s. “Darlin’, the lights will come back on. Gary and the department are dealing with it.”

“I…”

“Rayna. I love Elliot but he went a little overboard when it came to these things. You told me that yourself.”

“I know I did, but that was back then. I just thought it was him being overly cautious for when he was away on deployment.”

Jill snorted. “Do we have a shelter?”

"No, but…"

"Rayna. Gary is no different. He talked about potential disaster situations but he never built a shelter."

"You say that as if Elliot was crazy to do it?"

"No, but we know how things went with Elliot."

Rayna leaned back in her chair and frowned. She couldn't believe she had the nerve to say that. Was she insinuating that Elliot was crazy because he had PTSD? "Gary went through PTSD, Jill. He has many of the same symptoms."

"And he got through it."

"Oh so because Elliot didn't, that makes him less of a person? Is that what you're saying?"

Jill got up from the table and placed her cup on the counter.

"I'm not saying that. I…" she trailed off.

"What is it?"

Rayna could tell she was bothered about something. Jill gripped the counter for a few seconds and then turned towards her. "I know about you and Gary."

"What?"

"The relationship."

"What relationship?"

"Rayna, don't take me for a fool."

Rayna got up and placed her cup on the counter. She didn't like where this was heading or what Jill was accusing her of. But it seemed pretty obvious.

"You want to say something, say it."

"How long have you been seeing my husband?"

Rayna chuckled and ran a hand over her face. She cast a glance outside to where her kids were playing. "Let me ask you this, Jill. Have you ever brought it up with Gary? Have you ever asked him about this?"

"No."

"Maybe you should," she said scooping up her bag and heading to the back door. "Let's go, kids."

"But…" Lily said.

"I said, now!"

She could feel herself starting to boil. Jill looked over at her and opened her mouth but then closed it again.

Evan and Lily hurried towards her while Kong bounded behind them nearly knocking them over. They headed towards the front door and Rayna stopped with her hand on the handle. “How long have we known each other, Jill?”

“A long time.”

“Then you should know me better than that.”

With that said, she closed the door behind her and they set off for home. She didn’t fault Jill for bringing it up. She would have done the same but to assume that she was the one at fault, and then to get back at her by suggesting that Elliot was crazy, was a low blow. Her thoughts drifted to the past. In the time that Elliot was away on a deployment, it wasn’t uncommon for Gary to drop around and check in to make sure everything was okay. He would usually have a cup of coffee and they would catch up with what was going on in each other's lives. Sometimes he and Jill would invite her over for dinner a couple of nights a week but that was it. He’d never made a pass at her and to be honest she never got a sense that he was remotely interested.

That all changed two months after Elliot left them.

Gary would show up at all hours. Morning, afternoon, though usually it was in the evening. It was always the same. He wanted to talk about Elliot, find out how she was coping and see if there was anything she wanted done around the house. She should have picked up on it. He was overly interested and frequently visiting. But she just saw him as a close friend, nothing else. Then one night while Jill was away at her mother's for the week, she'd extended the offer of having dinner at her place as she didn't want him to have do all his own cooking. They ended up having a little too much wine and after the kids had gone to bed, he leaned in and kissed her. Of course, even in her intoxicated state she knew it was wrong and instinctively pushed him back and told him she was not interested.

He apologized and immediately left. There were a few awkward days after that but eventually it was smoothed out and things returned to normal — for a time. Then it happened again though this time she lingered in the kiss. She wasn't sure why she did it, but it was the worst thing she could have done. He took that as a sign that she was interested and from there on out, he took every chance he had to show his affection. She refused to lead him on and made it clear that if he wanted to remain friends, it had to stop. Thankfully he listened, and there was a good eight months when they didn't speak. It was difficult, but she had her morals and besides, she'd known Jill for far longer than Gary. She couldn't do that to her. After ten months passed, he was back at it again, though it was less obvious. A hand on the back. An extra visit in the week. A gift here and there. It was only a matter of time before Jill got wind of it. The town wasn't big and people talked, especially when they saw a police cruiser sitting in her driveway at all hours.

Jill must have assumed they were having sex, but that wasn't the case. She didn't want to ruin her relationship with Jill by telling her that her husband was coming on to her. How would that have made her feel? Would she have even believed it? Then again there was the fact that he was a cop. People in the town held them to a higher standard. Rayna also didn't want to jeopardize his career, so she tried to remain friendly but firm, making it clear that she wasn't interested.

She watched her kids run ahead. Kong bounded alongside them.

They were another reason why she didn't step over the line. Both of them adored their father, and it had cut deep when he left. If they'd seen her with Gary in an intimate exchange, they would have blamed her, and felt that she had played a role in Elliot leaving. She couldn't have that.

"Stay close," she called out as they ran ahead and veered off into the driveway. All the way home she'd noticed small groups were gathered discussing the problem and how to deal with it. Near her home there were some crowded around a lamp post that had a flyer attached to it. She stopped to read it. It was about the city hall meeting that night. The flyer, and the crowd distracted her as Lily emerged from their driveway yelling at the top of her voice.

"Mom! Come quick."

## Chapter 20

"It cost you how much?" Damon asked as Elliot weaved the truck around stalled vehicles. The vehicle had drawn a lot of attention over the past half an hour. They'd had to get out a few times to push vehicles out of the way. There were all makes and models, trucks, SUVs, sedans and even motorbikes clogging up the road. Not an easy job at all, and one that had already nearly lost them their vehicle after a group of three men tried to take it. Then on top of that, they had to deal with desperate people trying to flag them down. For Maggie it was hard to drive by them, but Elliot knew that stopping for anyone could get them killed.

"Just a little over eighty thousand."

"For a shelter? And what's that give you?"

"The bare basics. You can actually get different ones for a lot cheaper. There are small ones that cost around ten grand and give you a unit that bolts into a garage or your house. It provides two beds, a toilet and an air system. But that's bottom of the line and is only meant to protect you from fallout or a tornado. It would do the job but when you have kids, you're gonna need something bigger, especially if you are going to be in there a while," he said.

They'd got on the topic of how Elliot knew so much about EMPs and what steps he'd taken to protect his family. At first he'd considered not telling them, as he had a general rule of keeping everything hush-hush, but after all they'd been through together and the fact they'd probably come in handy to protect his family, he thought he could make an exception. Besides, right now he had no idea how long this was going to play out for. If it was a nuclear attack, fallout intensity would drop within the first two weeks. It was best to stay in a shelter for a month but if push came to shove, two weeks would suffice.

"So you have a Geiger counter at the house?"

"Yeah, it's in the shelter."

It was normal for people to be concerned about a nuke

dropping, however, there were a lot of variables that came into play. Did it hit the ground or detonate in the air? How far away was it? What size was the nuke? What was the weather and wind patterns at the time?

"Although fallout decays rapidly in the first two weeks, the closer a person is to the blast region, the more dangerous it is. Now my guess is that it occurred farther inland, and don't hold me to this but I'm assuming that it was a high-altitude detonation. Now again, I might be completely wrong. It might have been a solar flare that caused this."

"So how can we know for sure?" Jesse asked.

"I'll get on the ham radio once we get back and hopefully someone like FEMA is broadcasting a message."

"And if it's closer?"

"Well we might have radiation poisoning."

Jesse blew out his cheeks. "Great. And how would we know?"

"Depends."

"You keep saying that."

"Because it does, Jesse. This isn't some event that is black and white here. There are a lot of variables that come into play. Radiation symptoms will vary based on the dosage of radiation and the amount of time you are exposed to it. Everyone in the world is exposed to what they class as natural and artificial radiation through medical treatment, what we consume, and so on. The body can handle a certain amount a year but it's those large doses that we need to be concerned about."

"Okay, so let's say we have been exposed to it, what then?"

"Usually you will feel nausea, experience vomiting, diarrhea, headaches and fever, and that can happen anywhere from an hour to twenty-four hours after you've been exposed."

"So we might have been exposed to it and won't know until later today."

"That about sums it up. Obviously later you might start to feel dizzy, disoriented, weak and fatigued, all the way through to losing your hair, noticing blood in your vomit and having wounds that are unable to heal."

"Sounds wonderful," Damon said before chuckling.

"Again, it can take two to four weeks before those kinds of symptoms show up."

"And you know this because?"

"Learned about some of it in the army but take a look at Fukushima. They evacuated everyone within a 30-kilometer radius and said there was no threat in Tokyo which was around four hours away from the radiation. But remember that wasn't a bomb, it depends what has been dropped."

Damon sat there running his hand over his gun. "Eighty thousand? That's a lot of money to slap down on an underground shelter."

"It's what was available at the time. Like I said, there are cheaper ones. I think the last time I looked there was one priced at nineteen thousand and that was a multi-functional space under the house that could protect you from a bomb. It provided space so you could store food and water, a gun rack, bunk beds and give you a living space but again it's the bare basics."

"So what's in yours?" Damon asked.

"It's made from galvanized corrugated pipe, they install it for you. It has a primary hatch that is blast proof with an escape hatch on the other end. I had it built under my shed about twenty feet below the surface. There is a decontamination room that consists of a shower, then beyond that is a washroom with a marine-grade toilet that works on a hand pump, though I can have it gravity fed out. Beyond that are four bunk beds, a living area with a fully functional kitchen, then beyond that a double bed and below the floor is a storage area. It also uses a Swiss-made air filtration system to make sure the air is clean."

"You thought of everything."

"No, someone else did, and I just bought it."

Damon was just about to respond to that when Elliot eased off the gas. They'd been traveling north on Valentine Avenue. They had only seen three other older vehicles in operation and all of them were driving at a fair clip to avoid being stopped.

Up ahead on the left side of the street was a blockade being run by cops from the 46th Precinct. They'd blocked off East 181st and appeared to be randomly stopping pedestrians and checking them. On a street with no other vehicles moving, they were immediately spotted. They probably heard them long before they came into view.

"Shit," he said. Unregistered weapons, a stolen vehicle, yeah, they weren't going to get off lightly. Elliot jammed the gear into reverse, looked back and floored it. The tires squealed as the truck slalomed around stalled vehicles.

"Elliot, what are you doing?" Damon asked.

"You want to go back to jail?" he asked. He spun the wheel, and the truck slammed into a minivan. Coming down the road, three police officers were sprinting. Elliot gave it some gas and headed west on East 180th Street. No doubt they would have taken custody of any vehicle that was operational, but a stolen one? Spending time in a cell was the last thing he needed. The truck bounced as he took it up onto the sidewalk because the road was too clogged and they didn't have time to clear it. They headed down past Ryer Avenue heading for Anthony Avenue but that's when they saw another roadblock.

"Oh you have got to be kidding me!"

Elliot slammed the brakes on. Maggie looked over her shoulder and he eyed his mirrors. The cops were still coming after them on foot.

"We need to bail. Now!" Damon said pushing the door open and hopping out. "Come on."

Elliot gritted his teeth and slammed a fist against the wheel. He wished he'd taken a different route, headed over to Manhattan and tried heading north that way. There was nothing he could do about it now. All four of them bolted heading north up Anthony Avenue and then ducking into an alley down the side of a five-story apartment block. They entered the apartments and double-timed it up the staircase and into one of the floors, then waited for ten minutes until they knew the cops weren't following.

"They won't follow. They just wanted the truck,"

Damon said.

"So did we."

Elliot slammed his fist against the wall. At this rate he would never get home. He didn't think it would be this hard to leave the city but with society beginning to unravel, it was only a matter of time before police and the National Guard tried to keep the peace. That meant confiscating any vehicles that were operating, arresting those looting and making sure that gangs didn't take advantage of the weak.

Damon turned to Maggie. "You remember what you said about us showing up with bicycles? I guess that's plan B."

# Chapter 21

The front door was wide open. Rayna knew damn well that she'd locked the place before leaving. That was one thing she was a bit finicky about. Many times she'd get into her vehicle only to return and give the door handle another shake. It didn't look as if someone had forced the door open. The door, the handle, the frame looked fine.

"Lily, Evan. I want you to go over to Mr. Thompson's house. Tell him to come quickly or contact the police." She groaned. No phones were working and while Lake Placid was a small town, it was still spread out. Chances were they wouldn't see an officer around their part for some time if they were watching over the grocery stores.

"But Mom, what about you?"

"I'll be fine. I've got Kong. Just go."

The two of them clasped hands and sprinted off down the driveway, only pausing for a few seconds at the bottom to check on her. She waved them on before turning her attention to the house.

"Here boy," she said to Kong. He trotted up, and she kept her hand out. Her mind was racing as she started to think about the two men. If they were armed, she wouldn't be able to do anything. She'd returned the rifle to the cabinet before they left that morning. She scanned the windows and contemplated backing away, heading over to Mr. Thompson's and joining the kids. Elliot would have wanted her to do that, perhaps that's why she went inside. She couldn't rely on him now. This was her home, and no one was going to drive her from it. Quietly she got closer, keeping a firm grip on Kong's leather collar. Now she wished she'd had Kong trained to attack. Instinctively it was hard-wired in German shepherds to protect, but training would have made him even more responsive.

She pushed the door open, and it creaked a little. As soon as she stepped inside, she could see where they'd gained entry. The back window in the kitchen had been smashed in. There were shards of glass all over the floor.

She had only one agenda as she stepped inside and that was to get to her rifle, but that was located in the basement.

Kong growled and pulled a little.

"Steady, boy," she said. Upon entering the foyer, the living room was to her left, a flight of steps to her right, and the kitchen ahead. She glanced up the staircase. "If there is anyone in the house. You better leave now. I have a vicious dog and I will set him on you."

There was no response.

"I've already had someone go get the police. Again, if you are in the house, I advise you to make yourself known and leave now!"

She hurried down the hall and made a beeline for the basement. Not wasting a second she made her way down. As she got to the bottom, she noticed that some of the cupboards had been opened, and the drawers were on the floor. She stepped into the laundry room where the cabinet was and thankfully it was still intact. She pulled out the key and stuck it into the lock and yanked it open.

As soon as she had the gun in her hand, and had checked that it was still loaded from the previous night, she felt relief. A quick check of each of the rooms in the basement and she was satisfied. Kong shot up the stairs and she followed as he went about sniffing the floor. He dashed into her bedroom, then into the kids' as if he was tracking a rabbit. Rayna followed a few seconds after and held the gun out as she kicked open the closet doors and made sure that no one was inside. As she was finishing her search, she heard footsteps downstairs and then Evan's voice calling out. "Mom. We're back."

She called out to them to come up. Lily was talking rapidly to someone, telling them about the visitation they'd had in the night and that they were worried about being attacked.

"I bet you are," a male voice replied. As they rounded the corner and came up onto the landing she was greeted by Mr. Thompson who was red in the cheeks and looking out of breath. He was a tall, wiry man in his mid-sixties. Gray hair at the sides, bald on top, and he wore a thick pair of glasses. He was wearing a pair of black slacks, brown shoes and a thick coat because of the cold weather. He and his wife, Ivy, lived just one door down from them. All the houses were spread out so the chances of him actually seeing anyone break in would have been slim. Their home was surrounded by woodland. In fact all the homes along Mirror Lake Drive had been built on small plots of land that had been scooped out of the forest.

"Rayna, everything okay, dear?"

She exhaled hard. "Yeah. I'm sorry. It's a bit unnerving to come home and find out that someone has broken in."

"I bet. Well, you're not the first. Three houses were hit today."

"Really?"

He nodded. "We were home, thankfully." He looked around. "Did they take anything?"

"Doesn't appear so but I'm sure they got away with something."

She thought back to the two men, Austin and Trent,

who'd visited in the night. Had they planned on hitting the house at midnight? Had they broken into the other homes?

He nodded and sniffed, leaning a hand against the wall. "You going to the town hall meeting tonight?"

"We'll be there."

He smiled and looked at her gun. "Good to see you're packing."

"It's Elliot's."

He eyed her and studied her face. "I don't mean to pry, Rayna, but have you heard from him?"

She shook her head. "Nothing."

"That's unfortunate. He was a good man."

"That he was. Is, I mean." She corrected herself noting that she was speaking about him in the past tense.

He thumbed over his shoulder. "Well, I should head back. You sure you're okay?"

"Yeah, I've searched the house."

Mr. Thompson headed down a few of the steps before turning back. "You be sure to let me know if there is anything I can do. We need to stick together as a community. We'll get through this." She smiled, and he headed on out. "See you later, kids."

Just as he was going out she hurried down the stairs. "Mr. Thompson."

"Yes, my dear?"

"Do you have a generator to stay warm?"

"We sure do. You?"

She nodded. He waved and headed off down the driveway. With the power out, she knew it was going to affect the older generation first. With no heat, it wouldn't take long for some of the weak to get hypothermia, especially those in nursing homes. Her own father had passed away several years ago from cancer and her mother had followed a year after that from surgery complications. If they'd still been alive, perhaps she wouldn't have found the whole ordeal with Elliot so hard to cope with, but now she was alone, except for her brother and sister and well…

She thought back to that night. The blood. The phone

call. Gary showing up and the visit to the hospital. She pushed the event from her mind as it hurt too much to think about it.

Back inside the home she went about having the kids check to see if anything had been taken. Rayna entered the kitchen and began taking stock of what she remembered was inside the cabinets. She soon discovered that some food and water had been taken from the kitchen but that appeared to be it. Nothing else. They hadn't even stolen the generator. There was something very odd about the break-in. Why would someone break in and only steal a few items?

The TV was still there, so was some loose cash she'd left in a bowl on a side table. There was at least twenty-six dollars there. If they were druggies, they would have snatched it. She checked the medicine cabinet. That was all there.

It didn't make sense.

She glanced outside towards the shed and that's when she saw that the lock had been broken off. "No, no," she muttered bursting out the back door and hurrying across the yard.

"Mom, what is it?" Lily asked chasing after her. The padlock was on the floor, someone had taken a bolt cutter to it. She swung the door open, and the mat had been lifted up. A smile flickered on her face. They'd attempted to get inside but had failed. She could tell they had tried shooting at the flat lock as the only damage was to the paint which had chipped off the blast-proof hatch. Still, it wasn't good news. They might have failed, but they now knew she had a shelter and that meant there was a chance they would return.

## Chapter 22

It was early afternoon before they ventured down from that apartment. They'd remained there for the better part of an hour until Elliot was sure that it was safe to move on. Minutes earlier, Damon and Elliot had gone up onto the roof of the building and scouted out the maze of roads. From the roof of the six-story building it afforded them a good view of the concrete jungle and where the cops had created blockades. So far they hadn't seen any military presence, but there were a few buildings on fire, according to Damon.

"Distractions," he said. Attempts at luring away emergency services so people could loot stores, was the general consensus.

Before leaving, Elliot had doubled back to see if the truck was there. Of course, it wasn't, the cops were probably using it, but he had to check. They figured that it would be easier to find a couple of bicycles in the city than an older model vehicle, but until they were out of the Bronx, Elliot said it was best they stuck to hiking as vehicles and bikes only seemed to attract unwanted attention.

For the most part, people left them alone as they trudged north. On foot the journey of two hundred and eighty miles would take over four days; by bike, twenty-eight hours; and by vehicle, five hours. The journey would take them up around the Hudson River, through Albany and via Chestertown. That's why Elliot hadn't given up on finding another vehicle. Every old-looking truck, car or van they passed, he stopped at to check if they could get it working. This meant a lot of stopping and starting.

It was around two in the afternoon when they came across a bike shop on the outskirts of Kingsbridge. All of them were exhausted and by the looks of the store the owners had taken measures to ensure no one got in. The steel shutters were down, and two locks had been clamped into place with a warning sign.

Jesse looked up at the apartment above it and wondered if it was even worth it.

“So what do you want to do?”

“Well I can tell you what I don’t want to do,” Damon said, leaning against the wall and slumping down on his ass. He pulled his boots off and rubbed his feet.

“I’m going around back,” Elliot added.

“You did read the sign, right?” Jesse said, pointing to the warning about how attempts to break in would be met with extreme violence.

“It’s a ploy.”

“What?”

“No one puts up a sign outside if they are armed to the teeth. They have no reason.”

“Of course they do. They don’t want people tearing up the shutters with a forklift.”

Jesse frowned and tossed a hand up. “It’s a bike shop.”

“And that means it’s valuable. The bicycle was invented long before the car.”

He chuckled and headed around back. That was the

thing about Elliot, he marched to the beat of his own drum. It was like he didn't give a shit whether he lived or died. Now, Jesse had been the same way after losing Chloe. Heck, right up to the day of the blackout he would have willingly taken a bullet to the head, but something had changed in him after it all happened. It was like a wake-up call, making him realize how valuable life was.

"I'll go with him."

"You do that," Damon said. "I'll just rub my feet. Or maybe you can do it, Maggie."

"In your dreams," she said.

"Darling, I've spent eight months dreaming about it."

Jesse followed him around to a parking lot that was hedged in by a chain-link fence. At the corner of the building was a set of steps that went up to a door. They climbed them and then Elliot gave the door handle a try. It was locked. No surprise there. He then climbed out and up onto the top of the metal that covered the staircase, reached up and pulled himself up the wall onto the roof of the two-story building. Jesse followed him, convinced this wouldn't end well. Even though they hadn't seen any police in a while, his nerves were on edge.

"You're determined, aren't you?" he said as followed him over to a skylight. Elliot didn't say a word, he glanced in and pulled out his gun and used the butt to smash the glass. It dropped down about ten feet into a loft-style apartment.

"My kids are at home. I have no choice."

"But you left them behind."

"And?"

"It just strikes me that if you actually cared for them, you wouldn't wait until the shit hits the fan."

"I didn't."

"But you still left."

He shook his head and carefully climbed over the lip and dropped into what appeared to be an abandoned apartment. Once he was down he brushed off some glass that had embedded in his bicycle gloves and gazed around the spacious abode. There were large windows on either side of the building to let in a lot of natural light. Elliot must have been bothered by his question as he turned after reaching the door and stuck his finger in Jesse's face.

"You haven't got a clue what I've been through."

"Maybe not but I know I wouldn't have left my family behind."

"So what, you think you're better than me?"

He shook his head. "No. I'm not saying that."

"Then shut the hell up."

They made their way to the main door and were about to exit and head down a staircase for the store when they heard a man's voice bellow for them to stay right where they were.

"Don't move. You even breathe and I will drop you."

Both of them lifted their hands. Jesse knew Elliot was going to try something. He just hoped he didn't get them killed. Before he did, he thought he would at least try to get the guy to relax.

"We just need a couple of bikes," Jesse blurted out.

"And you thought breaking in was the way to get

them?"

"Well forgive me, but your store wasn't open," Elliot added.

"That's right. Because of headcases like you two. Now pay attention. You are going to exit, head down the steps and go straight out the door at the bottom. Do not enter the store. Do not pass go. Do not collect two hundred dollars."

Jesse frowned, then grinned. "Monopoly?"

"Go. Now!"

They hadn't even seen the guy's face. Jesse turned a little, and he was quickly told to look ahead.

"I've got money," he blurted out.

"And I've got a gun," the guy said making it clear he wasn't in the mood for a transaction. They were lucky they didn't get a bullet in the head. As they walked down the stairs, he kept telling them to keep their hands where he could see them. He hadn't checked for weapons which was either stupid or a smart move on his part. It could have gone either way.

"You a bike messenger?" the guy asked as they continued on down.

"Yeah."

"I recognized the clothing and sponsors. Who did you work for?"

"A few shitty companies. I doubt you've heard of them."

"We actually supply a number of messengers with bikes."

"Well maybe you can give us four."

"Four? Stop right where you are." They froze. "Where are the other two?"

"Outside."

Jesse turned. He knew he was taking a risk, but he got a sense through the questions that he wasn't going to shoot them and if he did, well, it wouldn't have been the worst place to die. He stared up the stairs at the man. He was in his late twenties, a bit of a hipster with a plaid shirt, a white V-neck, tight black jeans, designer specs and a beanie. He had a gaunt face and looked like he could have done with eating a burger or two.

"How many bikes do you have in this place?" Jesse asked.

He jerked the muzzle of his 9mm. "Turn around and keep moving."

"Look, man, my friend needs to get home to his kids. We've got a long way to travel and—"

"Do I look like I give a fuck?"

Jesse started laughing.

The man frowned. "What's so damn funny?"

"Two guys break into your apartment, hoping to take four of your bikes and you're here defending it at all costs like you're expecting the world to go back to normal."

"I don't expect anything. Now I'm doing you a favor. You can either walk out that door, or I'll put a bullet in both of you and not lose a wink of sleep tonight. Your choice!"

"Well now you put it that way, we'll be on our way," Jesse said turning back towards the exit and following Elliot out. As soon as they were outside, the steel door slammed behind them and they heard a bolt lock in place.

"Um, those look like some fine bikes," Damon said, still rubbing the bottom of his sole.

"Very funny, smart ass," Jesse replied.

"Let's keep on moving," Elliot said.

"Keep on moving?" Damon said as he rose to his feet. "I have a blister on the bottom of my toe, my thighs are killing me, and you want to keep moving?"

"Look, you want to stay here? Be my guest but we are wasting time."

"You were armed, and you didn't shoot this guy?"

"He had a gun on us," Jesse said. "What do you expect us to do?"

"And? So did the guy in the cemetery, and the one in Brooklyn. That didn't stop you then."

"He's just trying to protect his livelihood," Jesse said turning and continuing on a few more steps before looking back. Damon was staring up at the steps that led back to the roof. Without saying a word, he entered the parking lot and began climbing.

"Damon!" Maggie said.

"No, fuck this. The guy probably has fifty bikes in the store and he can't give us four? I've dealt with eight months inside a hellhole, come out to find the world gone to shit and now some asshole is trying to protect a few pieces of metal?"

Maggie looked at Jesse and he shrugged. "What do you expect me to do?"

"He'll get himself killed. Go after him."

He waved her off. "He's big enough to deal with it himself. I'm with Elliot on this one. We move on."

Elliot watched Damon climb up onto the roof like a monkey. He moved with purpose. "Actually, let's see how he does."

"Are you serious?"

He shrugged and hopped up onto the hood of a Ford SUV.

A few minutes passed and then the sound of gunfire erupted. It was rapid and then it stopped. Seconds passed, then the door opened at the bottom. Damon emerged with a straight laced face. "Well? You coming in or what?"

"You killed him?"

"No. I just gave him something to think about."

When they walked inside, the guy was sitting on the floor of his store without a weapon and uninjured. How the hell Damon had managed to pull that off was a mystery. Even after they rode off on four mountain bikes, Damon wouldn't say.

## Chapter 23

The bike ride out of the city wasn't an easy one. They would head north on U.S. 9 and then in the last few hours switch over to NY-73 Eest. Though he didn't know what he would say to Rayna when he returned, it felt good to be going home. He couldn't begin to imagine how much the kids had grown, and he was eager to see the look on Kong's face. Now that they had bikes, Elliot figured that if they didn't stop, they could be in Lake Placid within a day and a half, but that idea went out the window the more Maggie lagged behind. They had to stop so she could take breaks and that was only slowing them down. Along the way they saw all manner of vehicles stalled. Elliot stopped a few times to check a few but none of them had started up like that old truck back in the Bronx.

By late afternoon, they hadn't covered much in the way of distance, but they had managed to make it as far as

Kitchewan near the New Croton Reservoir. They decided to stop so Maggie could rest her leg and have a bite to eat. Damon was still griping about his toe. The only one who still looked fresh-faced was Jesse. "How many miles did you used to do, Jesse?" Elliot asked.

"Anywhere from 40 to 60 miles a day."

"So this must be a piece of cake to you?"

"Different kind of riding as I would stop frequently to deliver packages but yeah, overall an easy day, I guess."

"And before that?"

"Banking. Investing. Spent most of my day looking at the stock market. Helping people with their portfolios over the phone. Good money but hated being inside."

"That's why I joined the army," Elliot said biting into a banana and leaning back on a grassy embankment. They'd rested their bikes in front of them. Elliot had taken the higher ground so he could keep an eye out for trouble. They'd seen a number of desperate people along the way but they didn't stop.

"How many years?"

"Sixteen," Elliot muttered as he chewed. Once he was done, he tapped out a cigarette and lit up before taking a swig of water. They ended up refilling their containers from the river.

"Would you go back?"

"I'm not sure. I've thought about it at times, but it wouldn't be the same."

"Did you lose a lot of friends?"

"Everyone has."

There was silence as they took the time to recharge their internal battery. A cold wind nipped at Elliot's ears and a gray sky threatened rain.

"You said you have kids?" Maggie asked, squinting as she chewed on some peaches from a can that Jesse had brought along.

"Two. A boy and a girl."

"How old?"

"What is this, twenty questions?"

"Sorry, just curious."

He was hesitant to answer then he replied, "Fourteen

and thirteen."

"You must miss them."

"Every day."

He knew what she was going to ask next as the same thing had gone through Jesse's mind. Everyone wanted to know why he would walk away from his kids. It wasn't anything they had done, neither was it anything to do with Rayna. He loved her more than life itself but it was for their own safety. Time away had taught him a lot. It had allowed him to reflect upon what he'd been through. Listening to the group therapy sessions, even if he wasn't involved, had made him understand that he had done the best he could under the conditions. The horrible things he'd seen in Iraq weren't his fault. They were just part and parcel of war.

"What will you say when you return?"

"I've thought about that a lot over the past twelve months and to be honest, I don't know. I don't expect them to welcome me with open arms or accept what I did, but I did what I thought was best at the time for them, for me, for everyone." The three listened to him without passing judgment. It was easy to judge, harder to listen.

"Do you feel any guilt over killing those men back there?" Jesse asked.

He shot him a glance. "Well let me ask you this, do you feel any relief over being alive?"

That pretty much answered that and he expected him to back off but he didn't.

"No, I appreciate what you did, I'm just trying to understand what you feel when you take a life."

"Why?"

"Because maybe I'll have to take one."

Elliot scrutinized him before replying. "When you put it that way, sure, I'll answer you. No. I don't feel any guilt. When it comes down to it, it's either you or them and I can tell you right now, it will always be me standing."

Jesse nodded and took a swig from his bottle. He rolled his head around and got up and stretched. "You should all do it. Stops your muscles from cramping up."

Damon snorted. Jesse glanced at his watch.

"You still living by that?"

"Just seeing how long we've been on the road." He put his water bottle back in the bag. "It will be dark soon. We'll need to camp. We should get moving."

"Dear me, we only just got here," Damon said. "Slow down. You might be used to riding sixty miles a day but I'm not. I've been penned up for the last eight months. The only exercise I've seen is a few laps around the yard."

"So what was it like inside?"

"You don't want to know."

"I'm curious."

"Don't be. Curiosity is what killed the cat, and you strike me as a real pussy," he said before smirking. "Look, it's a different way of life inside. You have to keep looking over your shoulder. You don't really know who your friends are and you're never fully rested."

"So you should be able to cope with all this then," Jesse joked.

"I guess." He stared at him for a second or two. "Why did you change your mind?"

"What?" Jesse said as he slipped his arm into his backpack strap.

"You were going to stay in Brooklyn. Why did you change your mind?"

He glanced at Maggie, and Elliot smiled. The power of a woman. Of course, Jesse didn't say that, he cleared his throat. "There was nothing for me in Brooklyn. Anyway, I always wanted to visit Lake Placid."

"I bet you did," Damon said, a smile dancing on his face as his eyes bounced from Jesse to Maggie.

Maggie must have noticed as she frowned. "What?"

Damon gulped down some water and wiped his forehead with the back of his sleeve before getting up. "You got any more smokes, Elliot?"

"I'm afraid I'm all out," he said rising to his feet and preparing for the long journey ahead. Twenty minutes later they were back on the road, weaving around stalled vehicles, passing by strangers who looked on with a deer in the headlights look. Elliot kept the pace steady; he had to if they were to cover as much distance as possible. Maggie fell back a few times but did her best to keep up. As Elliot rode on, his mind chewed over the question Maggie had asked about what he would say when he returned. There were few things that scared him in the twelve months he lived under New York City's streets, and rubbed shoulders with drug addicts, but the thought of seeing Rayna again ate away at him. What if she rejected him? It wasn't like he was coming home to pick up where he'd left off. He knew he couldn't do that. For all he knew she might have been living with someone else by now. He wouldn't have faulted her if she'd moved on. Not once in twelve months had he contacted her, not even to say that he was alive and well.

The fact was Lake Placid hadn't been home in a long while. He wasn't sure how his kids would react or if they would even allow him to step inside the house. Was he a lunatic for believing that there was hope? Not just for his relationship with his family but for society?

## Chapter 24

"Brother, you are worrying about a bunch of nothing," Trent said to Austin. "I'm telling you, it's a fucking gold mine out here. The cops are too busy watching the grocery stores, the bank, the pharmacy, and God knows what else." He dragged the dead body of a man in his late fifties out of the living room into the kitchen. A trail of thick blood soaked into the carpet, then smeared on the vinyl floor as he dropped him before heading over to the fridge and taking out some milk. He gave it a sniff and chugged it back before spitting on the ground and tossing the carton across the room. "Shit, that is nasty!"

"Did you really have to kill him?"

"He was about to run out the front door. What did you expect me to do?"

Austin ran a hand over his head and exhaled hard. "This wasn't meant to happen. No one was meant to get hurt."

"And no one has."

Austin stared down at the floor.

"What the hell is that?"

"I don't see anyone and neither does anyone out there." He walked over and grabbed his younger brother around the back of the neck and shook him. "Austin. There are no cameras working. I haven't seen a cop down this road all day. And those fires we started on the far side of town, that's keeping them busy. No one is going to show up to check on the well-being of an old man. So fucking relax, you are getting on my tits," he said before pulling out a cigarette and sparking up. He blew a plume of smoke in the air and tapped his fingers against the counter. "Think about it. While all those idiots are out there trying to loot the stores, argue at the town hall tonight and deal with the cops, we'll be building our little nest egg, and tonight, that nest is going to grow a lot bigger after we hit a few more homes and then get that bitch to open up that underground shelter. I guarantee you, she has a huge stockpile."

"And what do you propose to do with her? You going to kill her too?"

He walked closer and blew smoke in Austin's face. He was only a year younger than him but wet behind the ears when it came to business. "I will do whatever it takes to survive. Mark my words, little brother. You'll be thanking me when they've run out food in the stores and we have more than enough to eat."

"And when the police come knocking, what are you going to say then?"

"Hello officer, can I help you?" He smiled. "No one has seen us. They're out there."

"She has."

"Well, we can remedy that quite easily."

Austin paced back and forth. "No, I don't like this. She has kids, a dog. You saw it yourself."

Trent reached around to the small of his back and pulled out a Smith & Wesson revolver and tapped it against the side of his temple. "Where there's a will, there's a way."

Austin sighed.

Trent shook his head. "If you're that worried, we can wear masks. So she's seen us at her place. There were a lot of people out last night on the roads. What, you think she's going to identify us in a lineup because we were concerned neighbors? Come on."

"I'm just saying it's risky."

"Grow some balls and get cracking. It will be dark soon and we still need to lug this gas and generator back to the house."

"What if the power comes up?"

"All the better."

"The police will be all over us."

"No, they won't. You keep forgetting, Austin. No one has seen us and those that do…" he cast his eyes down at the body on the floor. "Anyway, enough worrying. I was in contact with Magnus before all of this. He says he's going to speak to Cole about having us run the operation here."

"You want us to get our hands dirty with drugs?"

"It's not like you haven't done it before, Austin. What's the problem?"

"That was a little bit of weed. We're talking cocaine here."

Trent leaned back and eyed him. "And?"

"That's real jail time."

"We aren't going to be the ones selling it, you idiot. I already have a few people in mind so don't worry about it and anyway, chances are if they haven't got the power on by now, they aren't getting it back on. So focus on the task at hand."

As his brother went into the next room, he pulled out a small tin and popped it open. Inside was a baggie of coke. He emptied some of it onto the counter and used his fingers to make a line before snorting it up. He just needed a little pick-me-up. Something to get him through the next few hours. They both had grown up in Lake Placid, attended high school and bounced from job to job just trying to make ends meet. It wasn't like they hadn't given life a chance, but it didn't matter what he did, it never threw back a bone. The drug business was easy money. For the longest time they'd flown under the radar, but with the business of his cousin recently picking up in Keene, he knew Lake Placid was ripe with opportunity. They knew most of the dealers in town. They were little guys. All hot air and no action. He aimed to change that, well at least he had planned to until this shit storm. Now he was adapting, using what he could to his advantage until he could figure out how they could monopolize the town.

Right now it was a bit of a pipe dream. Police were still in operation and would be for some time unless… his mind wandered thinking of the different ways he could reduce the number of officers patrolling.

Trent wiped his nose with the back of his hand.

He cast a glance at his brother who was griping in the other room about blood on the carpet. Pulling the trigger was bliss. He'd never felt that much excitement. Killing someone was the closest thing he'd got to having an orgasm. And there was not a damn thing anyone could do about it. Tonight, he would take whatever the hell he liked, and God help whoever got in his way. He snorted a few more times, wiped his nose and headed into the living room to join his brother.

## Chapter 25

The town hall was packed that evening. Rayna didn't think that many people could cram into one place. Murmurs spread over a crowd of familiar faces as she stood at the back of the room holding onto Kong's leash. She couldn't help overhear the conversations people were having. All of them were concerned, some were even planning on taking matters into their own hands if they didn't get solutions. It was a mixed bag. The local emotions were running high and the pressure for the mayor to deal with the situation had reached its peak.

At the front of the room, multiple officers were on hand to keep the peace, some of them were volunteers, others city officials dressed in suits and doing their best to remain composed while the surrounding crowd waited for Mayor Hammond.

He eventually emerged from behind a curtain with Gary, and the police chief beside him. A generator could be heard churning in the background providing lighting and enough energy to power some electric heaters and a microphone. Hammond was in his late forties, balding, with a gut that stuck out over his belt. In all the times Rayna had seem him, he was in the habit of sweeping what remained of his hair over his nearly bald head, and if anyone approached him to discuss issues in the city, he would go red in the cheeks and sweat profusely. Today was no different. He stepped up to the microphone, adjusted his collar and tapped the mic. It let out a booming noise, then there was some high-pitched feedback.

"Okay, well welcome everyone this evening. I know you have a lot of questions about the blackout and concerns about what is being done. As you know I'm Mayor Hammond. For those of you here who have questions, I am going to ask you to hold them until the end otherwise we aren't going to be able to get through this as quickly as we would like. That would be very helpful. Now we all know that power outages can happen and when these events occur we usually can get back up and running fairly fast. That's because they are quite often related to a downed line here in the town. Now that's all well and good if it's something we can fix. However, the problem that we are facing is that there are no downed lines in the town, and it's simply a case that we aren't getting power delivered to us."

"Why?" someone shouted out.

"For those of you who don't know how the grid works, the generating stations produce the electrical power, that is then carried to demand centers and distributed through the lines to individual people like yourselves. It appears those generating stations are no longer producing power. The systems are fried."

An angry murmur spread across the crowd and a few people stood up and started pointing fingers at the mayor.

He put out a hand. "Please. Please. Take a seat and calm down."

"We won't calm down. You work for us. What is being done?"

"We will be using the Olympic Center as a central shelter for anyone who doesn't have a generator to come and stay warm. We are currently pulling together as many generators as we can find from local businesses but those will not be handed out and will be used in central areas, such as the nursing homes, the hospital, the school, Olympic Center and here at town hall. We however will be distributing flashlights to those of you without them, along with bottles of water, food and blankets on a case-by-case basis."

"Case by case? What are you on about? If there is no water coming out of our faucets where are we meant to get it? I paid taxes for a reason."

That caused a huge uproar as everyone agreed. Rayna could see how this could spiral out of control real fast.

"I hear you. You have valid concerns. However, please hold your questions until the end. Each of you should have received a leaflet when you came in the door. The information on there should answer most if not all of your questions about where, what, when and why. Now, moving on."

Someone laughed. "Moving on. Oh yeah, I bet you're moving on to a warm bed tonight."

Hammond ignored the man's jab and continued. "Please do not open your freezer or fridge unless absolutely necessary. It should keep your food frozen and cold for 24 to 36 hours if the door remains closed. After that period you may want to place frozen goods outside your homes. The cold weather should work to our advantage for a while. I also want to advise you against using any form of charcoal or gas barbecues, camping heating equipment, or home generators indoors. These are known for giving off carbon monoxide, which you all know can't be seen or smelled but can kill you."

"Tell us something we don't know!" Randall Weathers shouted.

A few people cursed at him.

Hammond did his best to remain composed, but she could see the sweat pouring off his brow. Gary stepped up to the mic to offer some moral support. He interjected to let everyone know that if they weren't going to remain civilized, they would be escorted out.

"While we know that some of you will opt to use candles, we want to caution you and remind you that it's best that you use proper candle holders. Also, never leave a lit candle unattended and be sure to keep it out of reach of your kids. And whatever you do, please blow them out before you go to bed." He wiped his brow with a small white handkerchief. "At the back of the room we are providing some crank radios which will be used to provide local information on the outage so you can stay informed. There is a frequency listed on the flyer that you can tune into. It may take us a while to get that operational but that is one of the initial plans. Of course if you have a ham radio that should work too."

Gary eyed Rayna at the back of the room.

"Has anyone even checked to see if anything is being broadcast by FEMA?" a woman at the front asked. The mayor turned his attention to her.

"We are working on it."

"Well, work harder!" someone yelled in the back.

"Now if you have questions, I'll take them one at a time. However, I will not cover what is already on the flyer. Please refer to that."

Rayna was the first to get her question answered as she put her hand up while the rest just bellowed out questions.

"Yes?" the mayor asked pointing to her.

"Protection. I'm not sure you know but several homes on Mirror Lake Drive, including mine, have been broken into in the past twenty-four hours. What kind of support will be made available by the police?"

The mayor looked to Gary, and he stepped up to the mic.

"Good question. Our aim is to continue to provide protection and maintain the peace throughout the outage, however, as you can appreciate, we are working at a bit of a disadvantage right now in the sense that we no longer have vehicles that are operating, so response times will be longer. We are currently gathering together a group of volunteers who will be helping us maintain order. Our first priority is to prevent looting of the grocery stores, pharmacy, the banks, and to ensure order is maintained at the local hospital as well as here. We also have to deal with the recent string of fires in the town."

"So does that mean no one is going to come out?" Rayna asked. "I might be able to protect myself but I have some neighbors who are in their late seventies. What are they meant to do?"

"Of course someone is going to come out. We will send an officer out this evening."

"That's not going to be much use," someone barked. "Unless the officer stays there, whoever is doing this is liable to do it again. Now I have a rifle, and if anyone breaks into my place I plan on using it."

"I can appreciate your concern, however as you know, New York is not a 'Stand Your Ground' state and all laws will continue to be upheld throughout this time. I would caution you against using deadly force and to seek out an officer."

Someone laughed. "I live thirty minutes away from the department. What am I supposed to do? Tell them to hold on while I go get a cop?" he asked in an angry tone.

The crowd started up again, this time people started tossing empty coffee cups towards the front of the room, causing several officers to move in and force some locals out of the building. And it didn't get much better from there. As soon as Rayna saw the mayor retreat with a look of fear on his face, she knew this was way beyond their control. They were going to need a lot of volunteers if they planned on maintaining order. Lake Placid Police Department only had a handful of officers, certainly not enough to deal with the two thousand plus residents spread out over two thousand acres.

"That's it for now," Gary said into the mic. "We will keep you updated."

The remaining officers were quick to move in and start ushering people out of the building. Disgruntled locals protested saying that it was not enough, but their cries were lost in the noise. Rayna was about to leave when

Gary slipped through the crowd and called out to her.

"A word, Rayna."

She told the kids to stay with the dog while she spoke with him.

"You mentioned someone broke in?"

"Yeah."

"Did they take anything?"

"A few cans of food but it wasn't that which concerned me. They tried to get into the shelter."

"How did they know about it?"

"I don't know. Maybe they were scouting the homes and saw me go inside? Maybe they knew about it?"

"But Elliot never told anyone, besides us."

"Well did you say anything?" she asked.

"No. Why would I?"

"How about Jill?"

"Jill?" He looked perplexed.

She sighed and shifted her weight from one foot to the next.

"Has she been in contact with you at all today?"

"No. I've been too busy."

"I went over there today and… how do I put this?"

"What is it, Rayna?"

"She knows about you and me. I mean, you coming on to me."

She wanted to make it real clear that she was not involved and that whatever Jill had learned, or seen, it was entirely Gary's fault not hers. Okay, maybe she had overlooked some early flirting, but most guys were like that whether they were married or not. At least the ones she'd met through her work at the museum.

His face went a slight shade of white. He exhaled hard and looked around at the thinning crowd. He pulled her off to one side so they were out of earshot.

"What did you say?"

"What do you expect me to say when your wife is accusing me of coming on to you?"

"So you told her…?"

"I told her nothing, Gary. That conversation is for you to have. I just expected more from her. You know, if you have problems in your marriage you should talk it over with her, not come to me expecting to find what you're lacking. I don't deserve that."

"I know."

"I could have told her, Gary, but I didn't. At no point did I tell her that you were coming on to me. I could have destroyed your marriage, but I don't think that's what you want otherwise you would have left her by now."

He reached out to her, and she pulled her arm away. "Enough. There is no you and me. And from now on, I would prefer that you don't show up without Jill."

"Rayna."

"I mean it. You wouldn't have done it if Elliot was here, would you?"

He stared back at her. "He's not here."

"Even more reason why you shouldn't."

She turned to walk back to her kids.

"Rayna, I will send someone out this evening to your place."

She tossed up a hand to acknowledge him but didn't

look back as she exited the place. Her head was swirling with the day's events and her nerves were on edge about dealing with another night alone.

## Chapter 26

Elliot stared down at the flat tire. Life just kept sending curveballs his way. He lifted the bike over his head and tossed it as hard as he could at the wall before painting the air blue with curse words. They had traveled another four hours north of New Croton Reservoir and were riding through the town of Hopewell Junction when he heard the hissing.

"I can't believe you were at a bike shop and you didn't take a bike repair kit with you," he yelled at Damon, just looking for someone to blame. In reality, it wasn't his fault. He was as much to blame for not thinking of it. All this time he'd always been the one to take the initiative because he'd been the only one he had to think about. Now he was joined at the hip and had projected his expectations of himself onto them. It didn't help that he hadn't had a cigarette in hours and was in desperate need of some nicotine.

"Um, I'm pretty sure I was the one who stuck my neck out on the line and helped us obtain the bikes. So if you want to blame someone, blame yourself!"

"Guys," Maggie said trying to intervene. "This isn't helping the situation. Anyway, I think we should stop for the night. It's got to be at least ten o'clock and my leg is killing me."

"I told you, you should have let me stitch it up."

"Elliot, you want to stop blaming people?" Jesse said coming to Maggie's defense.

Elliot backed up with his hands in the air. "I knew I should have just left you all."

Jesse chuckled. "Ooh, is that where we are at now? It's our fault you got a flat tire?"

Elliot ignored him and walked away. "We are less than twenty-one hours away from Lake Placid. I'm not stopping the night here."

"Okay, then how do you suppose we get there? Think logically about this, Elliot. We are tired. We have been on the road for the last four hours. Maggie is still bleeding.

Damon is tired and now we are one bike short. Now had you not lost your temper and thrown the damn thing at the wall, perhaps we might have been able to find a home that had a bike kit."

"Who gives a fuck!"

Jesse could tell he was seething but taking it out on them wasn't doing any good.

"You're in a hurry to get back. I get that. But let's face the facts. You haven't been back in twelve months. If they have survived that long without you, I think your wife can cope another twenty-four hours without you."

Elliot glared at him and walked a short distance away.

Maggie put her arm on Jesse's shoulder. "Leave him. He just needs to cool off."

"You're telling me," Damon said kicking up some loose rocks from the dirt.

It was strange to see the streets empty, and vehicles clogging up every inch of the road. Some of the doors were open. Baggage was strewn across the road. There were several on fire.

"Where do you think everyone is?" Maggie asked.

He scanned the street and there wasn't anyone to be seen. He figured in a small town, they might have implemented a curfew but in which case, where were the cops to enforce it?

"Stay here."

"Where are you going?"

"I'll be right back."

Jesse got off his bike and leaned it up against an antique store window. He jogged on down Church Street and took a left onto main street. Farther down he could see a fire burning and make out what appeared to be a blockade. Someone had pushed into place multiple vehicles but there was no one there. That was odd. He returned to the group as he didn't feel good about it.

"What did you see?" Maggie asked.

"I've got a bad vibe about this place. We should keep moving. Where's Elliot?"

"He just headed down First Street, said something about checking out some vehicles."

"Wait here, I'll go get him."

Jesse headed off jogging down Church Street and took a right onto First. He scanned the homes in the darkness. He could see light beyond some of the windows. The sound of generators churning away could be heard, in fact it was the only sound that could be heard.

"Elliot?" he called out checking each driveway as he passed them.

No response.

He didn't walk far down that road as it came to a dead end. Assuming he'd gone east instead of west, he turned to head back when without warning a bullet whizzed by his head. Had it been a fraction of an inch closer, it would have taken his head off. Instead it struck a window across the road and shattered it. Before he even had a chance to register where it came from, another tore up the ground ahead of him.

Instinctively he scrambled, zigzagging in the darkness across the road to the home closest and then ducking down behind a rusted-out sedan. Several more shots were fired tearing up the side of the vehicle. He got down on his belly, pulled his Glock and looked under the vehicle. In the darkness he could see the silhouette of two figures walking slowly across the road. Shit, his mind went into overdrive. There was no way he could get back to where Damon and Maggie were without being seen, so he cast a glance over his shoulder towards the house. There were no lights on but that didn't mean someone wasn't inside. Bringing his attention back to the men, he aimed and squeezed the trigger twice, then without even waiting to see which way they ran, he got up and at a crouch sprinted towards the side of the house. He pulled the storm door open and slammed his foot into the door, but it didn't budge.

Another round echoed and whizzed by him, the second bullet struck the storm door and he knew if he didn't get the hell out of there, he was going to die. He scrambled around the back of the house and fired at the window causing the whole thing to shatter. He jumped up onto the porch and carefully eased himself into the home. Inside it smelled musty. He'd entered the living room. The place was in a complete state. Nothing more than a few pieces of furniture, a TV, and the rest was covered in old newspapers and bowls of half-eaten food, along with microwave dinners. He heard voices outside, so he exited the living room slowly and cast a glance up and down the hallway. He wasn't sure where to go. Up, down or just wait for the men to follow. Who the hell were they? Why the hell were they shooting at him? And better question where were the damn cops when you needed them?

* * *

Damon was lying on the ground enjoying a moment of peace and quiet when he heard the gunfire. At first Maggie thought it was fireworks, then when it happened again she knew. He scrambled to his feet, pulled his gun and both Damon and Maggie made their way down to First Street. With it being night, they couldn't see a damn thing.

"Listen, stay here, keep your head down, I'm gonna go

and see."

Her pulse was racing as she looked for where she could take cover. There was nothing. It was just an open exposed area. No trees, or bushes.

"I'm going with you."

"No. It's too dangerous."

"Well I'm not staying here."

Damon gritted his teeth and nodded. "Stay low."

They slipped around the corner and made their way down the residential street until they reached a large bush outside someone's home. They ducked down and assessed the situation. In the distance they could see the silhouettes of three men fanning out. Damon turned to Maggie. "You know how to shoot a gun?"

"No."

"It's simple."

He quickly showed her how to load, unload, chamber a round and hold the gun. While it seemed simple enough, the thought of firing at anyone scared the shit out of her, even more than being fired at. She didn't want to kill anyone.

"Whatever you do, don't point that thing at me. Okay?"

She nodded.

They moved in silence, stepping over a small white fence that only came up to waist height. They slipped through someone's backyard, around a large round pool, then took cover by a red barn.

"Hold this position. I'm going to get closer but I need you to cover me, you understand? Anyone fires at me, you know what to do."

"Know what to do? I have no idea," she replied.

He just shook his head and rushed out into the darkness leaving her sitting there. The sound of more bullets whizzing by, tearing up the front of a house across the road, made her drop to her stomach and take cover. She gripped the gun tightly and frantically took in her surroundings. Under her breath she began praying. Please let me live. Please let me get through this.

* * *

Elliot was on his knees, blood trickling out the corner of his mouth while the stranger's gun was pushed up against the back of his skull. He'd been going from house to house when he came across a Jeep that he was certain dated back to the mid-seventies. It had been souped up, and they had changed out the wheels and pimped out the inside with leather seating and top-of-the-line audio equipment. He'd smashed the window and was in the process of hotwiring just like Damon had shown him when he heard a gun cock. Four guys dragged him out and began beating the shit out of him in the middle of the driveway.

If it hadn't been for Jesse calling out, he was sure they would have killed him.

Now three of them were out there hunting Jesse down while he was on his knees just waiting for this guy to get distracted so he could lash out. It hadn't been the first time he'd received a beating. With both hands resting on the ground and spitting blood, his mind drifted back to Iraq.

His platoon had been in the town of Rutbah when they came under attack. He and a buddy got separated from the group and took cover inside a home and came under heavy fire. After running out of ammo they'd been overwhelmed and dragged out, tossed into a vehicle and driven a short distance into the desert where they were thrown out and beaten with thick sticks.

Had the rest of his platoon not found them, they would have died out there and been thrown into an unmarked hole in the desert. Even now as the guy stuck the gun against his skull and told him not to move, his mind was reliving the past.

He could hear the insurgents screaming at them. He could feel each blow and see the look of pain on his buddy's face. Rage welled up in him, his eyes focused on the man as he moved around trying to see what his pals were up to. Every now and again he would call out the name Steven and then tell Elliot that he'd fucked up.

Oh he knew he had fucked up but the only thing on his mind was getting home. That was all that mattered.

He just wished he'd heard them approach while he was tucked under the steering wheel.

Elliot spat one more time, then reached down to his ankle for the blade he kept taped against his leg. They hadn't thought to check him as they probably were planning on putting a bullet in his head after the beating. That was a mistake. His fingers wrapped around the knife and in one smooth motion he twisted, knocked the guy's gun hand out the way and slashed him across the thigh with the blade. The gun went off, but it was too late. Within seconds it was over. Elliot was operating on pure adrenaline as he jammed that knife into the man's gut and ended his life in the middle of that driveway.

He spat on the dead man's face before getting up.

Not wasting a second he scooped up the Glock and hurried to help Jesse.

## Chapter 27

The officer Gary sent that night wasn't planning on staying. He did a quick perimeter search, took a statement and then moved on to the next house that had been burgled. It had been almost forty-eight hours since the power outage and already society was coming apart at the seams. It was subtle but beginning exactly as Elliot had said it would. Things would get worse from here on out, so Rayna was doing everything she could to protect herself and the kids.

"Why do we have to go inside there?" Evan asked.

"It won't be for long," Rayna answered.

"But we won't be able to breathe."

"Of course you will," she said ushering Lily down the steep steps inside the shelter. All the while she had one hand on the rifle and was eyeing the tree line around her property.

"Now Lily, I'm going to need you to reach up for

Kong when I lower him down." That was one thing the manufacturers hadn't given thought to when they designed these shelters — pets. Sure, it was easy to carry down a small cat or dog but Kong was close to ninety pounds, and there was no way in hell she was going to be able to lift him and they weren't going to leave him outside. So what she had done was wrap a sheet around his body to create a makeshift harness and she was going to lower him down and Lily and Evan would make sure he didn't bang into the sides.

It wasn't an easy task as Kong just thought it was a big game and he started to tug on the sheet, dragging her into a tug-of-war match in the back yard. If her neighbors had seen her, they would have thought she was insane.

"Come on Kong, knock it off!"

He growled playfully and tugged and hopped around, his bushy tail wagging away.

"Evan, go around and grab him."

One second she thought she had him, the next he ducked under her arms and was across the other side of the yard. In the end she had to put her gun down so she could corner him. Once she finally managed to wrap him up, he looked like an Egyptian mummy. Evan thought it was hilarious. To make sure she didn't drop him, she tied the other end to the top of the ladder and then slowly lowered him down while bracing herself against the ground and using her feet against the rim of the opening for support.

"That's it. Keep it coming," Lily said.

Eventually he made it to the bottom, and she breathed a sigh of relief. Snagging up her gun she scanned the yard one more time before heading down the steps and closing the hatch above her. The steel locked into place and she no longer felt afraid. It was quite noisy inside as the generator ran the air filtration system pumping in air from the surface then filtering it and filling the inside. Rayna made sure the kids were settled for the night before she logged on to the command center console that was set up to provide her with a view of the outside. There were three concealed cameras providing her with a steady stream of surveillance footage. Because it was night what she could see on the main screen was a hazy night vision green. Satisfied and leaving it on, she went over to the ham radio and pulled out a small pad of instructions that Elliot had left behind. She turned on the ham radio and went about checking the different channels for a broadcast.

Nothing came over the speakers except for white noise.

None of the frequencies he'd provided brought any news of what was going on or what had caused the event. It could have been a flare or a nuke, and if it was nuclear, they had to worry about fallout.

Rayna sighed and turned off the unit. She checked on the kids and made sure they were sleeping before she returned to the living area and picked up the notebook Elliot had left behind. It was full of useful information on surviving an EMP but he had taken most of the guesswork out of it by building the shelter. It was packed with nonperishable items, dehydrated food, canned and jarred goods. Below the floorboards there was a wide selection of grain, salt, cereal, powdered milk, peanut butter, jam, dried fruit and vegetables and two 2,500-gallon polyethylene water tanks full of water. More than enough to last them without having to leave the shelter.

She tapped the couch and Kong jumped up, curling up beside her like a warm water bottle. She laid back and as she continued to read her eyes became heavy. Within a matter of minutes she dozed off.

***

When she awoke, Kong was no longer on the couch beside her and he was barking furiously. She glanced at the clock. It was a little after midnight, so she'd only been asleep an hour.

"Kong. Kong!" she yelled, but he wasn't listening to her.

She got up and went over to the screen to see what he was barking at and that's when she saw them. They were wearing ski masks, but she knew who they were just by the color of their jackets. She hurried over to Kong and pulled him back and wrapped her hand around his muzzle to keep him quiet. Lily and Evan looked up from their bunkbeds.

"What is it, Mom?"

She put a finger up to her lips and they instinctively looked up at the sound of boots on top of the hatch. They could hear talking, it was muffled and she couldn't make out what they were saying but she didn't need to. One loud bang, followed by another and she knew what they were trying to do.

"Evan, take Kong to the back of the shelter, get your shoes and remain in there. Rip off a few sheets from the bed and tie them together. We might have to create a harness for Kong again. Lily, I want you to focus on the surveillance cameras. Tell me where they are." She nodded and hurried back. Rayna made sure her rifle was loaded and there was a bullet in the chamber ready to go. She aimed the rifle up and thought back to what Elliot had said.

*"No one is getting in. That door is blast proof. They only way they could enter is if they use a blow torch."*

"Lily, what's going on?"

"One of them has walked away and returned with a large bag."

"And?"

"Hold on a minute. I don't know, he's disappeared again."

"Find out where he's gone."

"I'm looking, Mom."

She was panicked and overwhelmed. It was one thing to be told about these kinds of situations, another to be in one. She was terrified but if they managed to get in, it wouldn't go well for them.

"Mom, it looks like a generator."

Rayna kept her eyes focused on the hatch for a few more seconds before hurrying back into the living area and over to where Lily was. She took one look at the screen and her heart sank. One of them had what looked like a grinder in his hand. Golden sparks were flying in the air as he tried to take off the hinges.

"Can they get in?"

"No, we're safe down here."

"But..."

"It's okay, Lily, your father knew what he was doing when he had this installed."

If they managed to get through the primary hatch, it would bring them down into the decontamination room. From there they would need to get through the laser cut-door that separated the decontamination room from the rest of the shelter. It was designed like a door in a submarine. It had latches which closed it off and it would protect them even if someone fired at it. It would take one hell of a job to try and get through there and even then, by the time they got through, they would be out of the escape hatch which was concealed and came out a few feet inside the tree line. On the surface it wasn't even visible. There was a system in place so that the escape hatch was buried about four inches under the ground. A quick pull of a chain and a hatch would open and sand would spill through and they could climb out.

Her mouth dropped when she saw them move from a

grinder to a blowtorch. A sharp blue flame sparked up and she could now hear the sound of hissing. They were determined to get in and she was determined to live. She grabbed up one of the two-way radios and hoped to God that Jill or Gary had turned theirs on.

## Chapter 28

Jesse's heart was pounding. What sounded like glass cracking beneath boots caught his attention. He brought up the Glock preparing himself for the fight of his life. Minutes earlier he'd crept upstairs fully expecting to startle the homeowner, but no one was in the house, or at least in the room he'd snuck into. It was a master bedroom with a large queen-size bed, flowery drapes, a closet and several side tables.

"You might as well come out," the gruff voice said. "We've got your friend."

He didn't respond. Sweat beaded on his forehead. In all the years he'd lived in New York City he'd only ever encountered one life-or-death moment and that was with those assholes who robbed him on New Year's Eve. Back then, he really had no fear of dying. He was so tired of living and missing Chloe, he wouldn't have cared if the guy had pulled the trigger and left him for dead. It would have been sweet relief to an existence that didn't feel whole or good. It was surprising how much this event had shaken him. It had rocked him to the core and made him think about who he was, what was important in life and… his thoughts went to Maggie. He couldn't believe he was thinking about her at a time like this.

"You know how this is going to end. Now if you come out, maybe we'll let you live."

He knew what they were doing. One of them was trying to get him to talk while the other tried to locate him. He peered out of the door down the corridor. It was pitch-dark. Not even the light of the stars provided any illumination. Jesse heard the sound of stairs creaking, and someone getting closer. He looked over his shoulder towards the window and considered climbing out. Then he had an idea. He slipped off his sneakers and padded across the hardwood floor and pried open the window. He pulled back the drapes, then quickly returned and got inside the closet. He squeezed himself into the corner and twisted the slats on the door so he would have a good view of whoever came through the door. He made sure he had a bullet chambered, and he held the gun close to his chest aiming it upright.

"You know, it doesn't have to end bad. Just come out and we'll talk about it."

Who were these people? How many had they done this to? Had they killed the occupants of the house he was in now? After seeing the way Elliot dropped those men back in New York City, he was certain now that there were those that would do anything to survive even if it meant killing a stranger.

Another creak.

They were getting closer.

Jesse took a deep breath. His hands were sweating. He tried to control his breathing but whatever calm he managed to experience soon vanished when the door opened. Any second now. His heart was beating so fast he was sure the stranger could hear it. A hulking man entered, his handgun raking the room, he then looked towards the window and hurried over to it.

"Steve."

"Yeah?"

"Check outside. I think he went out."

The sound of boots down below. The man turned and dropped down beside the bed, then as he got up he looked at the closet. Jesse swallowed hard. *Go. Get out,* he thought as he watched the guy skirt around the bed and get closer to the closet. The stranger unloaded three rounds at eleven, twelve and two o'clock then reached forward with one hand to grasp the door.

"Martin. You okay?"

He paused at the closet door.

*Don't open it. Don't!* Jesse thought.

Then he released it and walked out of the room. "Yeah, did you find him?"

"Nah, if he got out, he's gone."

The guy walked out of the room and Jesse heard him heading across the corridor. He waited a few more minutes before he reached up and opened the door on the closet. Sliding across the ground he stayed low and peeked around the corner. He was still on the second floor going through the next room. Jesse contemplated making a run for it, but he knew the other guy was on the ground floor. It was too risky.

He moved back as the guy came out of the room. Did he see him?

He heart was slamming inside his chest as he heard his boots approach. Fuck.

Then, just at the last second, he must have turned and headed down the stairs as he heard boots on the steps.

Five seconds, ten seconds, twenty, he counted off in his head before taking another look and then slipping out. He heard the sound of glass crunching down below and figured the men were leaving. A wave of relief hit him, and he was about to head down when he passed the bathroom. A dark figure exploded out, smashing him into the wall, causing the gun to drop. It was the same guy. He must have heard him and was waiting for him to emerge.

Back and forth across the corridor they jostled, slamming into the walls.

"Steve?" the man below called out.

Jesse had a hold of the guy's wrist and was smacking it against the wall to get him to drop the gun but it wasn't working. The guy headbutted him, and everything went dark for a split second. Driven by adrenaline and a will to survive, Jesse forced him back into the bedroom until the back of his leg butted up against the bed causing him to lose his balance. He fell on top of Jesse and they rolled off the other side of the bed. Now Jesse was below and he was on top.

The gun went off in his hand, firing a round into the wall.

He had hold of Jesse's throat with one hand and was trying to bring the gun around so he could aim it at his head, but it wasn't working. Jesse reared his knee and jammed it into his groin as hard as he could, then thrust him back with both legs sending him toppling over. Bouncing up to his feet, he charged the guy, who was now on the ground, by driving his knee into his face.

Downstairs a gun went off, once, twice, then a third

time.

His attacker managed to get up and crack Jesse across the jaw. His head jerked to the side, but he wasn't out of the fight yet. He drove his shoulder as hard as he could into him, knocking him back through the open window. Both of them went out, toppling head over heels down the roof's incline and then over the edge.

When Jesse landed, it knocked the wind out of him. He coughed and spluttered and looked to see where the guy had gone. He was a short distance away and in the same pain as him. A few feet from him was the gun. Jesse rolled over trying to get to it, but the guy was doing the same thing. His hand clamped onto it before Jesse could reach it and he lifted as Jesse lunged forward. They rolled, and the gun went off.

## Chapter 29

There was no answer on the other end of the two-way radio. "C'mon!" she yelled causing her kids to become afraid. She looked at them and saw the terror in their eyes. Another glance back at that surveillance video and she knew they would eventually get through. Hot molten metal dripped down inside. She hurried over to the main door and closed it using two large latches to lock it in place, then returned to her kids. She was torn on what to do. On one hand, her best chance of survival was to stay inside but on the other, if they got through that hatch with the blowtorch there was no telling if she could hold them off with the rifle. On the other hand, she could wait until they were inside the decontamination area, then get out via the escape hatch but then they would have to get Kong up and that wouldn't be a quick or easy task.

She picked up the two-way radio again. "Pick up."

Nothing.

She couldn't believe this was happening to her. It seemed like a surreal nightmare.

"Mom..." Lily began to say something but Rayna was too focused on watching the two men at work. Anyone who would take the time to bring a blowtorch to a shelter wasn't going to give up until they got inside even if it took them an hour. Where the hell were the police? She wished she'd taken Jill up on her offer if only for the sake of the kids. The shelter provided a false sense of security. Certainly it was better than being in a house but still, she felt like a trapped animal. She knew the main door would hold them for at least an hour, maybe more and they still hadn't got through the main hatch, but she could see he was now working on the second hinge.

Thirty minutes passed, and they weren't letting up. The men stopped once or twice so they could take turns but that was it. When one of them was working on the hatch, the other would have a cigarette and would head off to check that no one was coming. She could see him walk around the house, out to the driveway and look either way then return. This time when the guy who referred to himself as Trent returned, he turned on a flashlight and began browsing the perimeter. What was he doing? He trudged through the long grass and appeared as if he was looking for something. Then she exhaled hard. No. He had found the two air vents. He banged on them a few times and the noise echoed inside the shelter. While she couldn't hear his voice, she could see him calling out to his buddy Austin. Austin put the blowtorch down and joined him. He was pointing to the air vents. Austin nodded and headed off around the house.

"What are you doing?"

Trent brought his mouth up to the air vent and began yelling, that's when she heard him. "Hello down there! Wakey wakey!"

All three of them and the dog looked up at the ceiling.

"I'm growing a little tired of trying to get in that hatch. They don't make it easy, do they?" He took a puff on his cigarette and blew it out. "So here's what I'm going to do. You open up the hatch and come on out, and we'll let you go on your way. No one needs to get hurt here. All we want is what is inside. Okay?"

Was he expecting them to reply? Rayna walked over to the air filtration system. She could disconnect it in two areas if need be in order to hook it up to a separate filtration system just in case of a biological attack. Right now all that was being pumped in was the air from outside.

Trent continued. "Or we can give you a little motivation."

He took a deep drag on his cigarette and breathed out, down the air shaft. Then he looked off to his left. Austin came over with the portable generator and a large tube. It was quite clear what they were about to do. They were going to hook up the tube to the generator's exhaust and feed it down into the air supply. While Austin got it set up, Trent went over to the second air vent and stuffed several rags inside of it.

Rayna cast a glance at the air filtration system. It could handle nuclear or biological but carbon monoxide? She hurried over to the notebook on the counter and looked through it for details about the air supply. She eyed the video and could hear Trent yelling down to her to make up her mind.

She flipped past the page and then thumbed it back over. Her finger ran down the list until she saw it. She had the capability to shut off the outside source of air for up to six hours because during the first few hours of a nuclear attack, smoke, carbon monoxide, and radiation particles could enter through the air intake. However, as she continued reading, she came to the instructions on how to hook up the air intake so that it filtered through the large canister to prevent contaminants from entering.

Hurrying over to the unit, she went about setting it up using the quick disconnects and then stepped back from the unit. Her eyes darted over to the video. They'd never tested it out but if there was ever a time it needed to work, it was now. There was a carbon monoxide detector inside. She knew that the threat would build quickly in a sealed-off area if any escaped. Her eyes scanned the device waiting for it to beep.

Outside Trent shrugged. “Well, don’t say I didn’t warn you.”

He nodded to Austin, and they fired up the generator.

## Chapter 30

Jesse didn't even realize he was holding his breath as he rolled off the dead man. In the heat of the moment he had completely forgotten about the second man. A figure burst out of the house, and he reached for the gun. He was just about to squeeze off a round when he heard his voice.

"Whoa! Don't shoot, it's me," Damon yelled.

Jesse lowered the handgun and looked up into the sky.

"I killed the other two."

Damon walked over and extended a hand. He clamped onto it and pulled him up.

"Close one, huh?"

"Too close," Jesse replied. He cast one final glance down at the dead man, scooped up his gun and shoved it in the small of his back before heading around the front of the house. As they emerged, Elliot was coming across the road, his hand still holding the bloodied knife. His face had been battered and blood was streaming down from the corner of his eye.

"You look like shit!" Damon said.

He groaned. "I feel like it."

From farther down Maggie came into view. She hobbled over and reached up to touch Elliot's face but he winced and pulled back. "Everyone okay?"

"I could use a change of underwear but besides that, I'll survive," Jesse said casting a scowl at Elliot. "I hope it was worth it."

Elliot gripped his ribs. "It was. I've got wheels."

Jesse turned back and raised an eyebrow. "As in more than two?"

Elliot chuckled and jerked his head towards the house he'd come from. When they made their way over, he looked down at the body with multiple stab wounds. It was a sick sight. "I was in the middle of hot-wiring it when…" He thumbed towards the vehicle and Damon slipped underneath to work his magic. "Yeah, I haven't quite got the hang of it," he said before groaning through gritted teeth.

A few minutes later Damon brought the engine to life. He tapped the front of it and smiled. "Three-quarters of a tank. I'd say that's good news."

"Let's get the hell out of here."

They climbed in and Maggie took out some bandages from Elliot's backpack and used them to clean him up and cover the wound on his forehead. It was red, and swelling, no doubt he would have one gnarly bruise by the morning. Damon backed out of there and tore away. With a vehicle, they were now looking at it taking them less than four hours to reach the town. They passed through numerous towns, some that were in an even worse state than Hopewell Junction. It had been a hellish day of hiking and biking. They stopped once on the way to refuel by siphoning a couple of vehicles but that was it. Elliot had made it clear that no matter what, whether it was a gang, the police or even the army, they were to keep going and for once no one disagreed.

Jesse looked in the back after two hours of driving and

saw Maggie sleeping, her head leaned against Elliot who was also out cold. The warmth of the vehicle was lulling each of them to sleep.

"You want me to take a turn driving so you can get some sleep?"

"Sure, if you want."

He veered off to the side of the road and they swapped over.

As Damon came around he asked, "How does it feel?"

"To drive?"

"To have killed someone," Damon said, hopping in and putting his feet up on the dashboard.

He gave the engine some gas, and they pulled away driving on through the night. To be honest, he really hadn't dwelled on what had happened. It wasn't like he was trying to kill the guy. The sad fact was that it could have been him lying back there.

"I could ask you the same?"

Damon glanced at him. "You're dodging the question."

"Um." His eyes flitted to his rearview mirror to see if Elliot was awake. "I don't know. I don't feel anything. No remorse. No guilt. Is that wrong?"

"No. He did try to kill you."

"It's not just that. I…"

"You haven't processed it."

"Well, have you? Was that the first time you killed someone?"

He cleared his throat and looked out into the blackness of upstate New York. All they could see for miles were the silhouettes of evergreen and barren trees reaching up like gnarled hands, and vast farmland with large barns. Some of it was covered in a thin layer of snow the farther north they went. All of which reminded him of how tough it was going to be to survive the winter without heat.

Damon piped up. "Yeah. It was the first time."

"Are you just saying that to make me feel better?" Jesse asked.

He chuckled. "Just because I did time inside, it doesn't

automatically mean I killed anyone. And in answer to your question, I feel the same way. No guilt or remorse but maybe that will change in time."

That was what worried Jesse. He could handle a lot of things but guilt, even if he had fought back in self-defense, guilt could crush a man. He cast a glance at Elliot in the rearview mirror wondering what demons he was wrestling with. Had it come from killing others, seeing others die or both? And if it affected Elliot enough that he would walk away from his family, what effect would it have on him?

"When you get back, what are you going to do?"

"See my lady, have a few words with a friend of mine," Damon said.

"Same guy that put you in the situation that landed you inside?"

He nodded and stared out the window.

"You think he did it on purpose?"

"I guess I'll find out once I return."

No more words were exchanged between them.

Damon closed his eyes. Jesse gave the engine some more gas, and they drove on through the night.

# Chapter 31

"Why isn't it working?" Trent said pacing back and forth. They'd been pumping in fumes from the generator for the last hour and that bitch still hadn't emerged. Trent glanced at his watch while Austin crouched beside the generator staring at him.

"These things have an air filtration system on them which can handle carbon monoxide."

"What?"

"Yeah, they're designed to withstand a nuclear fallout or biochemical hazard."

His brow furrowed. "Why didn't you say that?"

"Because you didn't ask."

He cursed and kicked the generator and it spluttered.

"Shut the damn thing off."

Austin reached over and turned it off. "Then there is the chance that it did work and she's dead inside, which means we just wasted one hour."

Trent looked as if he was going to blow his top. He trudged over to the blowtorch and was about to spark it up when he threw it down and came over and pushed Austin back. "We didn't waste an hour. You did." He jabbed his finger into Austin's chest. "I can't believe you let me go ahead with that knowing full well that she could survive down there."

"I told you this was a stupid idea in the first place but oh you wouldn't listen to me. You always have to be in control. Admit it, you're a control freak." He pushed him back. "Now I say we leave now. She hasn't seen our faces."

Trent ripped off his ski mask. "Now she has."

"Huh. You really are stupid. I'm done."

Austin picked up the generator and began lugging it back to the truck when he heard a gun cock. "Don't make me do it."

He turned and frowned. "You going to shoot me, brother?"

"I will if I have to. We are in this now. You walk, she

talks, it's as simple as that. No, we use the blowtorch and keep working away on this. Eventually we will get through."

Austin dropped the generator and charged over to him and grabbed him around the neck. "Eventually? The sun is going to come up soon. Neighbors are going to be out. Police will be patrolling if they aren't already. We don't have more time."

He held him tight giving him a look of death. It hadn't been the first time he'd threatened his life and it probably wouldn't be the last, but he wasn't going to have him screw everything up.

"She's seen my face."

"You don't know that," Austin said.

"Think about it. If they design these things to withstand a shit hits the fan event, you can damn well expect they have cameras."

Austin looked around.

"And don't go trying to find them. They are probably concealed."

He released his brother.

Trent continued. "This thing would have an escape hatch, right?"

"Possibly. So?"

"Well think about it. It's only an escape hatch if you can get out of it fast. Which means it's probably not like the one we are trying to burn our way through. If we can find that, we might have our inroad."

Austin brought two fingers up to the bridge of his nose. "You just told me not to go searching for the cameras, but now you want us to search for the escape hatch? Are you out of your mind?"

"Listen. I will keep going with the blowtorch while you search the grounds. It has to be around here somewhere."

Austin ran a hand over his head and gazed towards the house. He blew out his cheeks then pulled out his flashlight and nodded. "Get to work then. I'll see what I can find."

His brother got this grin on his face as he returned to

the blowtorch and fired it up. He brought goggles down over his eyes and went back to work. Austin figured that the hatch could be anywhere within a 360-degree area. There was no telling which way the shelter was facing so he started on the north side of the shed and walked forward, keeping the flashlight on the thick foliage and banging his foot against the ground. He didn't know a lot about underground shelters but he knew enough to know that if there was an escape hatch, it wouldn't be that far underground and it would either be exposed or covered by a few inches of soil.

He just hoped they'd be able to find it before the sun came up.

## Chapter 32

Rayna had been studying the CO2 detector ever since they'd started pumping that crap into the air intake tube. To say she was beyond relieved that Elliot hadn't cut corners would have been an understatement. He'd paid for the best air filtration system on the market and right now it had just saved their lives.

Her heart was still hammering in her chest.

It wasn't over. It wouldn't be over until they were gone. Until the cops had arrested them. She stared down at the two-way radio and tried again.

"Come in, Jill, Gary?"

There was only static that came back.

"Mom, they are back at it again," Evan said pointing to the monitor.

She hurried over and stared at the multiple screens. One showed Trent working on the hatch while the other one was searching the grounds. "What are you after?" she mumbled.

"What's he looking for, Mom?" Lily asked.

At first she wasn't sure and then as she watched him banging his foot on the ground, she realized. "He's searching for the escape hatch."

"Can he get in if he finds it?"

She didn't respond to that but hurried through the shelter to the back and climbed through the tunnel and looked up. She looked at the notebook and thumbed through trying to find more details on the escape hatch. She knew that all she had to do was pull the chain and all the sand above it would drop down allowing them to go up but she was unsure about the lock mechanism. Was it as secure as the main hatch or weaker? Rayna began to pace. Her mind churned over. They were getting in one way or another. If they found the escape hatch, and they got through the main hatch, what then? She only had the one gun, and she had her kids to think about. She needed to get out and fast but how? Stay, leave, no matter what she did, she put her children at risk. Her panic level had reached a new height. Rayna kept going back and forth as she formulated a plan. She stared at the display and watched the two men. What if she created a distraction? Made them believe she was going to come out while her kids exited through the escape hatch and ran to get help? No, if they spotted them she wouldn't be able to live with herself. She'd have to go with them. At least that way she could protect them with the rifle. But then there was Kong. She looked down at him. If they exited, they wouldn't be able to get him up in time.

Another hour passed.

"Mom. You need to see this," Lily said.

She'd been in the back of the shelter looking up at the escape hatch contemplating how much noise it would make if the sand dropped. According to the notebook, there was only four inches between the surface and the hatch.

"What is it?"

She didn't even need to look at the screen as she heard his boots coming down the steel ladder. It echoed inside the shelter's chamber. He was whistling to himself.

He'd breached the main hatch.

"Well, well, well, look at that!"

She could hear him loud and clear now. He banged with his fist against the final door that separated them from him. Kong rushed forward growling at the door.

"Come out, come out, little pigs. Or I'll huff and I'll puff and I'll fucking kill every one of you!" His voice got louder and Kong started barking. The cameras weren't inside the shelter so she couldn't see what he was doing but she knew. The familiar sound of hissing meant the blowtorch was on again.

"Mom," Lily grabbed her mother's hand.

"Okay, listen up. We are going to make a break for it."

"No, he's out there," Evan said pointing to the screen.

She took hold of him and looked directly into his eyes. "I'm not going to let anything bad happen to you. You understand?" She saw his eyes well up. "Do you understand?"

He nodded.

"Lily, take your brother to the back room."

"What about Kong?"

"Kong is going to have stay here for now."

Evan pulled away from his sister with tears in his eyes. "No. I'm not leaving him here."

"You listen to me. Kong will be fine."

She didn't know that but as much as she loved that dog, her main priority was the safety of her family. Rayna waved for them to go while she went over to the door and tried to get the attention of Trent on the other side.

"Hey! Hey!" She had to shout real loud because of the noise of the blowtorch but eventually he heard as it went quiet on the other side, then he replied.

"Yes?"

"If we come out, you let my kids go and you can have whatever you want inside."

"A bit late for that now, isn't it?"

"That's the deal."

"Lady, there is no deal. You've already seen my face."

"They haven't."

"Don't bullshit me," he replied.

There was silence for a minute. "We just need to gather a few things together. Then we'll come out but I need your word that you will let my kids live. They haven't done anything. They're just kids."

"We were all just kids once," he said. "No deal!"

And like that the blowtorch came back on and now she could see a small hole forming. It was glowing a deep orange. Shit. Shit!

She hurried back towards the rear of the shelter and cast a glance at the screen. Her mind was moving at a million miles an hour trying to make connections, trying to think about how to do this. She considered just staying inside, waiting it out and when he came through the door shooting him but the odds were stacked against her. She couldn't take the risk. No, the only way was to get out.

"Listen up, Lily, when I say go, you pull that chain and step out of the way. Sand will drop down and then I want both of you to go up that ladder and to run through the woods to Mr. Thompson's house. You understand?"

She nodded.

"No hesitation and you do not wait for me."

"But Mom—"

"Lily!" she snapped with tears welling up in her eyes.

Rayna made sure the rifle was ready, she slung it over her shoulder and cast a glance at Kong. "We'll come back for you, Kong. I promise."

His head cocked, unable to understand them.

"Mom, we can take him with us."

"There isn't enough time. You remember how long it took to get him down. No. He stays."

She turned her attention back to the screen and waited until Austin was on the far side from the escape hatch before she gave Lily the go-ahead. Everything happened so fast. There was a whoosh as sand dropped, then she saw both kids hurry up the steps. Her eyes remained focused on the screen to see if Austin had heard.

He hadn't.

She turned and bolted towards the steps, her eyes focusing on Kong. She didn't want to leave him but she had no other choice. As she climbed, she looked down and saw Kong looking up. She tried to push the thought of him from her mind but it was killing her. That dog meant the world to her. As soon as she emerged from the shelter, she swung the gun around and was pleased to see the kids had sprinted into the woodland heading in the direction of her neighbor's home.

The problem was, Austin had heard them.

"Trent!" he yelled hurrying towards her kids, jumping over fallen branches. He hadn't even spotted her yet as she was still crouched down by the opening. She brought up the gun and did her best to aim and then squeezed off a round.

The crack of it echoed in the silence.

It didn't hit its mark.

Austin took cover behind a tree and glanced out, then returned fire. She scrambled for cover in the dense forest, knowing full well that at any moment now Trent would be coming up those steps and then any chance of her escaping with the kids would be over. In the distance she saw Lily and Evan stop and turn around.

"Go!" she screamed, then watched as they continued on.

She brought the rifle around and squeezed off another round as Austin darted between the trees trying to make his way over. As he got closer, she noticed Trent emerge with a handgun. He fired off a round and darted into the forest to join his brother in hunting her.

## Chapter 33

When the Jeep rolled into Lake Placid, it was three in the morning. Elliot had taken over driving an hour ago. He was relieved to see the familiar sights of his hometown and yet overly anxious to see his family. It wasn't a surprise to see no one out. The weather was freezing cold and like many of the towns throughout New York State; he imagined they had already issued a state of emergency and enforced a curfew.

As he veered left off Sentinel Road onto Main Street they practically drove into the blockade. There was no time to slip down a different street or even back up. A large floodlight came on, blinding him. He eased off the gas and brought his window down. Over the hum of the Jeep he could hear a generator. Cutting into the bright light came two figures walking towards him. He could already tell by their silhouettes that they were cops. Their duty belts, hats and hands on their weapons made that obvious.

Elliot squinted and held a hand up to his eyes.

"Driver. Shut off the vehicle," a male voice bellowed.

He turned off the engine, and they got closer.

"Take out the keys and put them on top of the vehicle."

They were treating him like a common criminal but it must have been odd to see a working vehicle rolling into town. He knew they wanted to use it and no matter what he said, they would take charge of it.

Gary had seen him before his eyes adjusted.

"Elliot?"

The familiar sound of his friend's voice put him at ease.

"Gary."

"Holy crap. I'll deal with this."

"But sarge…"

"I said I would deal with this. Now head back," Gary said to the other officer who was scrutinizing him. For a few seconds they looked at each other not saying anything. Gary shone his flashlight into the vehicle and over the faces of the rest of them.

"Who are all these people?"

"Long story."

"Where the hell have you been?"

He smiled and winced a little. His jaw was still hurting from the beating.

"You look like shit," Gary muttered.

"You don't look too good yourself, buddy," he replied. Gary stepped back from the vehicle and looked it over.

"I'm guessing this isn't yours."

"Nope, but…"

Before he could finish, Gary put a hand up. "Don't even tell me."

"Gary. Rayna. Is she…?"

"She's okay. At least she was when I saw her earlier this evening."

"And the kids?"

Gary studied his face before he sighed. "They're fine."

Elliot nodded and looked ahead towards the blockade

that had been set up. They'd shut off the glaring light and his eyes had now adjusted and could see four officers and two volunteers.

"Are you here to stay?"

"For now," Elliot said.

Gary's lip curled a little, and he placed a hand on Elliot's arm. "It's good to see you again, my friend."

"You too."

"You know we're going to need this vehicle."

"It's all yours as soon as I get home."

He nodded. "Bring it by tomorrow."

"Will do. How are things?"

"Not good but we'll get through it."

He chuckled and shook his head then tapped the vehicle. "Go on, I'll deal with the questions here. We'll speak later."

"Thanks, Gary."

As he started up the Jeep he looked over at him then smiled. He'd often wondered how Gary would react when he returned. He never imagined it would be under these circumstances. Gary had them clear the way so he could drive through town. It was a short distance remaining, less than five minutes. His heart began beating rapidly the closer they got as he veered onto Mirror Lake Drive and drove on through the final stretch.

# Chapter 34

Gunfire echoed. Rayna dashed from one tree to the next, sweat pouring off her brow. Her hands were clammy and her throat dry as she tried to keep them from pinning her in. She eyed the house and considered sprinting for it, but it would have meant running out of the trees and that was the only thing keeping her alive.

"You are really starting to piss me off, lady!"

To that, Rayna fired another round in his direction then fished into her pocket and loaded a few more bullets into the Winchester. The evergreen trees surrounding the property created a canopy that blocked out what little light came from the moon and stars. She laid herself down behind a tree and rested the rifle on a thick root, observing the two men darting in and out. They were getting closer and if she didn't take one of them out soon, they would be on her. Although she'd been firing at both of them to keep them back, she now focused her entire attention on Austin who was closest.

“It didn’t have to end this way,” Trent yelled.

She never responded to anything they said. It would have given away her location and in that moment that was the only thing working for her. She brought the rifle up as Austin made another dash to the next tree. She watched how he moved and waited until he shot out again before she squeezed the trigger.

This time she didn’t miss.

His body spun, and he dropped.

“Austin!” Trent darted out then ran back as she fired another round, this time at him. She looked over at Austin, he wasn’t moving. She’d been firing at them for the past ten minutes and not one round had hit them. It was just a matter of timing and the odds eventually swung in her favor. At least now she stood a chance. A new sense of confidence flooded her being as she loaded the gun again and prepared for Trent to stick his head out. *C’mon, you bastard!* Rage welled up inside of her at the thought of them attempting to hurt her children.

He dashed out, jumping and zigzagging until he reached his brother. She fired off a few more rounds hoping to get him now that he was out in the open, but he laid down close to the earth using his own brother as cover.

Silence crept over the woodland, nothing more than the sound of an owl.

Then she heard him weeping and saying his brother's name over and over again.

"You are gonna fucking die," he bellowed furiously.

Her senses went into high gear as she aimed the rifle and fired a few more times, then moved position. As she was running towards the next tree, she heard the crack of a gun, and felt a hot searing pain in her leg as she collapsed. Breathing hard and fast, she reached down and gripped her leg.

A moment of distraction and he was on her like a lion on a gazelle. She fired one last time, but he kicked the gun out of her hand and leapt on her, clamping his hands around her throat. She gasped for air and pounded the front of his chest with both fists but that only angered him more and he lashed out, catching her with two hooks to the jaw.

"I'm going to take you to the brink of death then bring you back and do it again, and again and when I'm ready…" He reached around and pulled a huge hunting knife from a sheath. "I'm going to gut you like a pig."

He placed the knife back into the sheath and she fought him with every ounce of strength she had left but it was useless, he was too strong and the pain in her leg was overwhelming. His hands clasped around her throat and she could begin to see darkness creeping in at the sides of her eyes.

Then everything went black.

A sharp stinging sensation and she was back again gasping for air only to see his face looming over her. "Welcome back, bitch!"

He squeezed again. "Die! Die!" he screamed as he applied even more pressure.

Then, there was a crack, red mist hit her face and

Trent slumped to one side.

Rayna gasped for air, sucking in as much as she could.

Frozen. Dizzy. Struggling to get air through a windpipe that was bruised and damaged by his grasp, she remained there motionless. Seconds passed and then she saw him.

"Rayna."

She squinted unable to believe it.

Was she dead? Was this some dream?

"Elliot?"

Then just like that her world rushed back in. The memories of the past. Her kids running to Mr. Thompson and the final few minutes of what she thought was going to be the end of her life. Elliot clamped hold of her hand and brought her up to a sitting position. That's when she saw others: a woman, two males and… behind them running across the yard with Mr. Thompson were Lily and Evan.

Elliot turned and saw his kids and their pace slowed from a run to a jog, then a walk. "Dad?"

Evan was the first to run at him, wrapping his arms around him and crying into his neck. Lily followed. Seconds turned to minutes and slowly she regained the strength to try and stand. Her leg was in agony and bleeding badly. She was full of questions but Elliot told her that now was not the time.

Behind them they heard a dog barking.

"Kong?" Elliot asked.

"In the shelter," she said jerking her head towards it. "You'll need to go through the escape hatch as it's still locked down below."

Elliot looked at her and she told him to go and get the dog. She stumbled a little as they emerged from the woodland and Mr. Thompson, told her that he'd had his grandson bike down to alert the police.

* * *

Elliot hurried over to the escape hatch and peered down. He smiled as the large face of his old friend looked up at him. At first it looked like Kong was confused then his tail started wagging and he began barking like mad.

"Yeah, yeah, I'm coming."

He made his way down the ladder and the second his boots hit the ground that big old dog jumped on him knocking him back and licking his face like mad.

"Kong. Kong. Stop. Stop," he said laughing. It took several minutes before he could work his way out from underneath the large furry mass. Kong then started whining and rubbing his head against Elliot's leg.

"Yeah, I missed you too, boy."

He wiped a tear that streaked his cheek before exiting the shelter through the main hatch after getting a little assistance from Damon to bring the dog up. Once up they entered the house and waited for the police to arrive. As Elliot listened to his kids' voices, and tended to Rayna's wounds, he looked up at her and realized how crazy he'd been to leave them behind. Sure, PTSD had been a struggle, and it would continue to eat away at him, but he now knew the only way to overcome it was to face it head on, with those he loved.

When he left, he wasn't ready to deal with it.

He thought the answer was to run from the pain.

To leave behind those who he didn't want to hurt.

"I'm sorry, Rayna, for everything."

She didn't respond as he treated her leg but eventually she replied, "You know, he pulled through. He didn't die that night."

A flashback of that final evening hit him. *Being inside the liquor store, seeing two armed robbers try to take cash from the register and her brother, Keith entering as the gunfire erupted. For the past twelve months he'd pushed down the memory and blamed himself. But he had no control over the hallucinations that came from his PTSD back then. When it all happened, he thought he was in Fallujah, caught in a fire fight.*

*That was until it was over, and three men lay bleeding on the ground.*

"He's alive?"

She nodded. "I never got to tell you because you left, but I don't blame you, neither does he." He felt himself becoming choked up and as he stopped to wipe the tears from his eyes, she leaned forward and put her hands around his head and pulled him close. She never said any words but her action did.

As the sun came up that morning, spreading its warmth across Lake Placid, the full scale of what they were facing became evident. Rayna was taken to the local hospital to be treated and Gary brought Elliot up to speed on what they were dealing with and the challenges that lay ahead. The situation was dire and the future bleak. Although they had overcome insurmountable odds trying to weather the past few days, the obstacles seemed even greater now. All of them realized that Austin and Trent were only the beginning of something far worse and even more deadly. As from panic to chaos, the world had begun to unravel.

* * *

## THANK YOU FOR READING

Days of Panic: (Book 1)

Days of Chaos will be out in February

## A Plea

Thank you for reading Days of Panic. If you enjoyed the book, I would really appreciate it if you would consider leaving a review. Without reviews, an author's books are virtually invisible on the retail sites. It also lets me know what you liked. You can leave a review by visiting the book's page. I would greatly appreciate it. It only takes a couple of seconds.

Thank you — **Jack Hunt**

## Newsletter

Thank you for buying Days of Panic, published by Direct Response Publishing.

Click here to receive special offers, bonus content, and news about new Jack Hunt's books. Sign up for the newsletter. http://www.jackhuntbooks.com/signup/

## About the Author

Jack Hunt is the author of horror, sci-fi and post-apocalyptic novels. He currently has three books out in the War Buds Series, Two books in the Wild Ones series, three in the Camp Zero series, five books out in the Renegades series, three books in the Agora Virus series, one called Blackout, one called Final Impact, one called Darkest Hour, one out in the Armada series, a time travel book called Killing Time and another called Mavericks: Hunters Moon. Jack lives on the East coast of North America.

Made in the USA
Middletown, DE
16 March 2018